WE WILL BE CRASHING SHORTLY

WE WILL BE CRASHING SHORTLY

Hollis Gillespie

MeritPress | fw

Published by
Merit Press
an imprint of F+W Media, Inc.
10151 Carver Road, Suite 200
Blue Ash, OH 45242. U.S.A.
www.meritpressbooks.com

ISBN 10: 1-4405-6770-0
ISBN 13: 978-1-4405-6770-4
eISBN 10: 1-4405-6771-9
eISBN 13: 978-1-4405-6771-1

Printed in the United States of America.

10 9 8 7 6 5 4 3 2 1

This is a work of fiction. Names, characters, corporations, institutions, organizations, events, or locales in this novel are either the product of the author's imagination or, if real, used fictitiously. The resemblance of any character to actual persons (living or dead) is entirely coincidental.

Cover design by Sylvia McArdle.
Cover images © Pavlo Kovernik/123RF; tshooter/123RF.

This book is available at quantity discounts for bulk purchases.
For information, please call 1-800-289-0963.

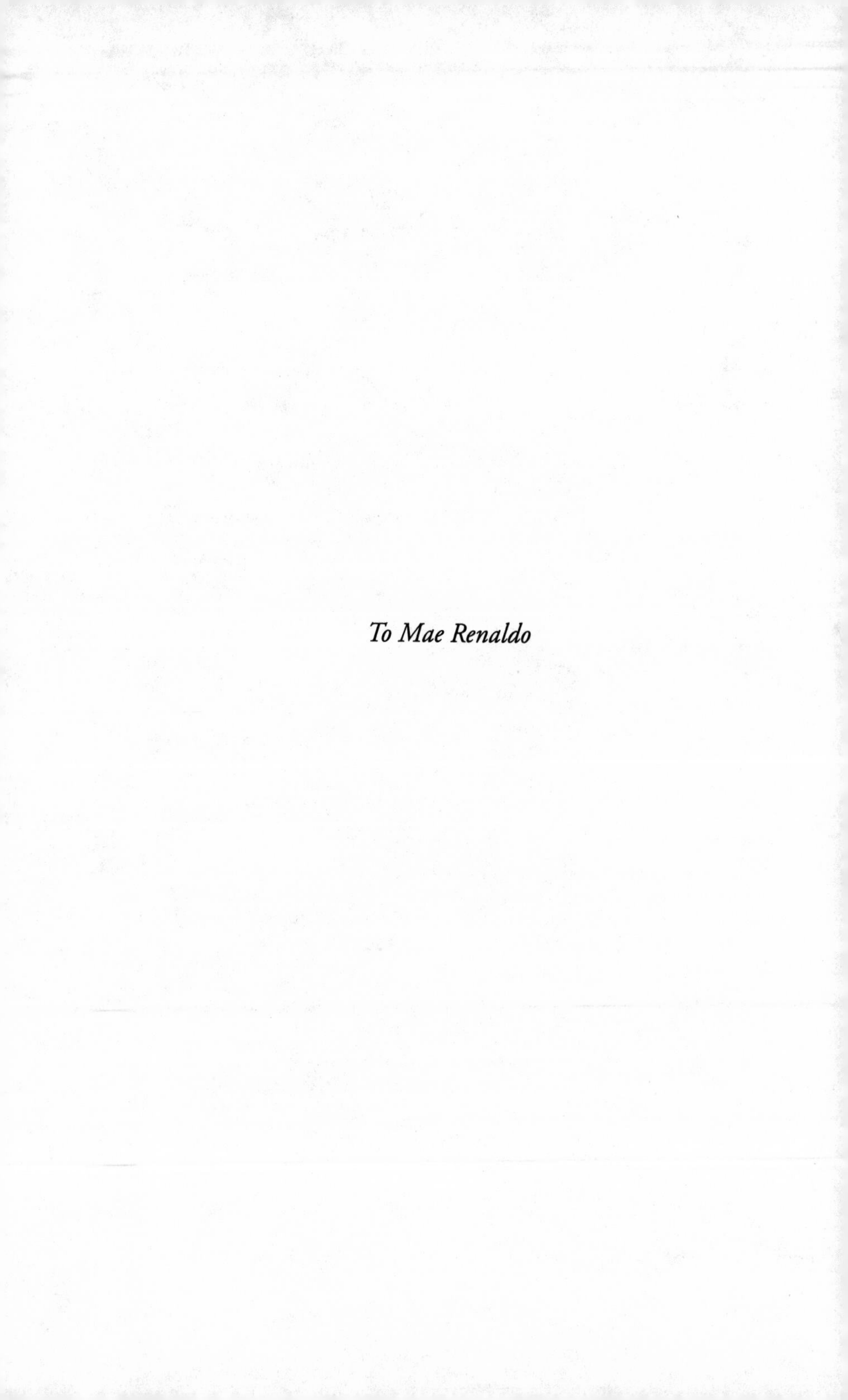

To Mae Renaldo

ACKNOWLEDGMENTS

Thank you, Jacquelyn Mitchard, for refusing to let me give up. And thank you, Grant Henry, Lynn Lamousin, Lary Blodgett, and Michael Benoit, for allowing me to study you as amazing human specimens. And thank you, Polly Biasucci, Kate Hicks, and all the other big, bombastic, lovely senior flight attendants from the nineties who let me live among you all those years. I have never encountered such a strong, hilarious, flexible, seen-everything, surprised-by-nothing, boozy, partying, life-loving, adventurous, capable, accepting, intelligent, incandescent, and independent group of women in my life. You can't fathom how fortunate I feel to have been allowed to be a part of that era with you.

CHAPTER 1

The last time I saw Mr. Hackman he was dead, but not decapitated.

I thought it was important to point that out. Because here I was hiding out while being sought in connection ("alleged" connection) with two homicides, and I wanted to emphasize the kind of killer I'd make if I were one, and if I were one I would not go around chopping off the heads of people like Mr. Hackman, an airplane mechanic whose guts I couldn't stand. I'll give you one of the reasons I hated him (and this is just one): His wife Molly, one of my favorite waitresses at the Waffle House, was still in the hospital in a coma, where he put her because he was a wife-beating son of a bitch.

I probably should have called the police right away. But I'm miserably aware of the public nature of 911 calls these days. Eight months ago I called the police when I came home to find my stepfather rummaging through my mother's files. Normally this would not have been alarming, but my stepfather was supposed to be in prison, or at least it was my understanding that prison was where they put fired WorldAir pilots who bombed planes. Evidently I was wrong.

It seemed like that 911 recording ran in the news on an endless loop for days afterward. The worst was the *Southern Times.* The headline read, "Deposed Airplane Princess Places 911 Panic Call, Shoots Stepfather." I did not shoot my stepfather, by the way. Not with a real gun, anyway. I used a paint gun. I thought it would assist the police in catching him—what with the easily identifiable, giant yellow splotch on the man's crotch—but then when the police arrived they just let my stepfather go. Today I was still stupefied over that.

So no, I did not cut off Mr. Hackman's head. Nor did I immediately (or at all) call 911 that day in the airplane hangar while I stood over his dead body. Instead of calling the police, I thought it would best serve the situation if I ran away and hid in the cargo bay of a nearby L-1011 until someone else came along to discover the body.

But this is not to say I didn't kill Mr. Hackman. I'm pretty sure I did.

"Are you certain? Are you absolutely positive?" Officer Ned asked. He seemed really concerned about me. He'd tried to reach my mother, who was on a cruise ship with my grandparents off the coast of Antarctica, but the most he could do was send a fax and trust it made it to her cabin. I suppose it was saying something that he had yet to call the real police and turn me in, considering they—along with the rest of the world, it seemed—were looking for me.

"Yes," I told Officer Ned. "I'm certain."

Officer Ned is a 6'5" former professional linebacker with legs like rockets. He could chase down a cheetah, he is that fast. (I've seen him tackle a fugitive on the airport tarmac even though the bad guy had half a runway head start.) He is African American, has a nice smile if he's so inclined (which he isn't often); he keeps his hair cropped close, his suits impeccable, and his vintage motorcycle boots constantly on his feet. And all five of his bullet wounds have healed nicely, thank God. Officer Ned was also my best friend, or one of them anyway. Two of those bullet wounds he got while saving my life.

Recently, due to circumstances that would seem fortuitous, he became the head of security at WorldAir, the largest international airline in the country. This was due in large part to me, seeing as how I owned the airline at the time. A very short time.

Now here we were, Officer Ned and I, in Hangar North 90 sitting in the dark cargo bay of the same L-1011 under which Mr. Hackman died. It's also the same L-1011 that we crashed in Albuquerque last April. WorldAir brought it back to Atlanta first to forensically investigate the damage and then to Frankenstein it back together by using another L-1011 that ran off the end of the runway a few years back. That plane lost its nose, and this plane lost its tail. Bing bang boom, glue the two together and get one good as new . . . hopefully. One thing they have yet to repair, though, is a hole in the bulkhead of the lower galley. That hole leads to the luggage belly and then to the floor hatch that accesses the cockpit. It's easily obscured with a strategically placed meal cart. I know about this hole because I put it there, and Officer Ned helped me do it. I also knew that if I was patient he'd eventually know where to find me.

"April, please," Officer Ned exhaled shakily and rubbed his temples with one hand. The other hand he reached over to take mine in his. "Start from the beginning."

CHAPTER 2

I'll start from the beginning. My name is April Mae Manning. I'm 16 years old (in a few days), the progeny of a long lineage of blue-collar airline employees, product of a bizarrely broken family, former runaway, former flight attendant impersonator, and victim of circumstances. Those circumstances include, but are not limited to, an evil stepfather and an engineer/inventor grandfather who left me a giant inheritance that included controlling stock in an international airline. Here is a piece that ran in the news about me last year:

Southern Times

"Teenager Credited with Saving Flight 1021 is Forcibly Removed from WorldAir Offices"

by Clay Roundtree

Entertainment Section, December 10, 2013

The FBI credits 15-year-old April Mae Manning for the survival of all passengers aboard hijacked WorldAir flight 1021, which on April 1 was crippled by a bomb, an incapacitated pilot crew and zero cockpit radio communication. Though there were no passenger fatalities, among the crew there was one flight attendant and one air marshal fatality, as well as one hijacker.

"If it wasn't for that kid, we'd all be just a red streak on the side of a mountain somewhere," John Porterdale, 53, a passenger on the fateful flight, says of Manning.

"This is all very much still under investigation, so I can't comment on any details of the hijacking right now," informs Anthony Kowalski of the Federal Bureau of Investigation. When asked to confirm reports that Manning was responsible for reconnecting cockpit communications in the ailing L-1011 aircraft, Kowalski simply answered, "That kid is a hero."

Until recently Manning was considered to be the largest shareholder at WorldAir, due to the estate she inherited from Roy Coleman, then believed to be her paternal grandfather, who died in 2009. In an odd twist of events yesterday, Manning was forcibly removed from the airline's executive offices after authorities confronted her with a subpoena from the Supreme Court compelling her to provide a DNA sample.

"It's best for everyone's safety that we take these steps to determine the truth behind any allegations of broken lineage between Mr. Coleman and Ms. Manning," says WorldAir spokesperson Rand Appleton.

Manning will be stripped of her seat on the board until her DNA conclusively connects her to Coleman's, whose remains are scheduled to be exhumed from Tolomato Cemetery in St. Augustine, FL, next week. Coleman's late son, Robert Madison Coleman, until recently believed to be April Manning's biological father, was cremated and is therefor unable to provide conclusive DNA material.

"We just want to be thorough," added Appleton, "especially in light of recent events."

Recent events include the disappearance of WorldAir flight 0392, which vanished from the radar over the Pacific Ocean on its way to Hawaii from Sydney, Australia, on November 18. After an extensive search using vessels dispatched from fifteen surrounding countries, nothing has been found of the plane or of the 267 passengers and crew within it.

"It's like it evaporated into thin air," says Walter Munson, a former investigator with the National Transportation Safety Board (NTSB). "There was not even a single cellphone ping to help triangulate a location. An entire 747 aircraft, just, poof."

At first I was beloved by the media, but then of course my popularity hit a point of diminishing returns. No surprise. For one, I'm not all that chirpy; I don't trust the media, the police, lawyers, judges, or bureaucrats. Then when the Supreme Court very publically granted WorldAir permission to seek proof of my paternal lineage, suddenly I was the "alleged" and "self-proclaimed" heiress to the company. Because it doesn't matter what you said or whether you actually said anything at all—if positive things are published *about* you, you will be credited with having said it. I swear it's true, and it's crazy. Not a single article ever printed contained a real quote from me. But now that the pendulum of public attention has swung the other way, suddenly I'm the "suspected imposter progeny of Roy Coleman" while my mother was expected to prove she didn't sleep around.

The first I even heard of this turn of events was when I was taking the driving test to qualify for my learner's permit. As I pulled out of the Atlanta DMV, which was housed in a double-wide mobile home across from Turner Field, suddenly my car was accosted by a gaggle of reporters and "citizen journalists" (an oxymoron if I ever heard one).

"Pull over!" the instructor insisted. "Now!"

I gunned it instead. Most of them got out of my way, except Clay Roundtree of the *Southern Times.* I tried to frighten him into moving, but the only person I frightened was the DMV lady assigned to assess my test. She screamed like a fishwife, grabbed the wheel, and slammed us into a tree. The move smashed the passenger-side front bumper, accordion-style, of the car my uncle Otis had leant me for the occasion.

The DMV lady stumbled out of the car clutching her neck and demanding the contact information for the owner of the vehicle. I gave it to her but no lawsuit was filed, probably because Otis began dating her the day she called him for his insurance information.

The car, by the way, was a seventies model BMW 2002. You would think it'd been in perfect mechanical condition, considering Otis is an actual mechanic for WorldAir. But it was already so beat up that the crash actually realigned the frame from former wrecks and made it drive better.

"This is fabulous," Otis shouted over the grinding of the gears. He'd seen the melee on the news on the television in the break room at the airplane hangar, and had gotten a coworker to drive him to the DMV and drop him off so he could scoop the car off the tree and take me home. "It's like you gave the car a chiropractic adjustment!"

I was really glad to see him, because I had been stuck there for nearly an hour. The crowd of reporters had been bolstered by news vans and even helicopters, and had gotten so big I couldn't break through to walk back to the DMV to cower in a stall of the filthy ladies bathroom. So I simply sat with my back against the tree, pulled my knees to my chest, and prayed the vultures would dissipate—a futile hope. Again, actual *helicopters* were involved.

Gawker.com had the biggest field day with that one, although no one, not even Clay Roundtree, could wrestle a quote from me. "How's it feel to know that the CEO of the company your grandfather left you suspects you're the bastard child of an illicit union?" he shouted as I struggled to close the passenger door shortly before Uncle Otis peeled us away from there. When the piece appeared on the *ST* website later, Mr. Roundtree had dubbed me "Crash Manning," a name that has stuck ever since.

"I like it," Otis grinned. It was a tad scary when he grinned like that. My uncle Otis was an impervious, booze-addled, arguably certifiable genius, and actually my great-uncle once removed if you want to get specific. He was also a former pilot, having worked for Pan Am for just one year until he became one of the few survivors of the infamous Tenerife airport disaster of 1977. To this day it remained the deadliest accident in aviation history, caused by a simple miscommunication between Spanish air traffic control and the pilot of a KLM 747.

"It was not just a simple miscommunication," Otis always corrected people about that day. "There were *many* factors leading up to it. Nobody ever mentions the bomb anymore." He was right, of course. (Otis is rarely wrong about airline information.) Earlier that day, a bomb had detonated at a nearby airport, causing traffic to be diverted to Tenerife in the midst of a dense fog. The pilot of the KLM 747 understood he had clearance to take off, which he attempted to do while another 747—the one my uncle was in—was parked on the runway. The resulting collision annihilated both planes and killed everybody aboard the KLM flight plus all but 61 people aboard my uncle's plane. Otis doesn't talk about it much until he's drunk, and then the details come out.

"The fog was dense like chowder, completely impenetrable," he'd slur after half a bottle of Jägermeister. "The conditions were terrible for traffic, but perfect for terrorists. Everyone was on edge."

Selfishly, I love to listen to him talk about it. Otis was deadheading at the time, sitting in the cockpit jumpseat behind the two pilots. He could hear the communication between the doomed KLM pilot and the control tower. "I remember thinking, 'Shit, that guy thinks he's cleared for the runway!' We all heard it. We could see their lights coming toward us."

On the cockpit voice recorder, you could hear Otis urging the captain along with the copilot and engineer to hurry off the runway. "Get off! Get off!" he cried. The captain did what he could to move the mammoth aircraft out of the way, but a 747 in a dead stop is no match for one barreling at 180 mph. All the survivors were found in the front section of the aircraft.

Otis lost his left eye in the accident, which canned his piloting career. He left Pan Am after that to join WorldAir as a mechanic, a move several steps down for him, and he never piloted a plane again. Today he kept a collection of glass eyes in a bowl by his sink, but normally eschewed them in favor of a black eye patch. Maybe it was this rogue-pirate effect that explained his evident irresistibility with women. I couldn't tell you how old he was because he had a face like a leather saddle, but it worked for him. I put him somewhere in his sixties, but youthful, like a blond Keith Richards, and with a giant toothy smile like that creature in the *Alien* movies.

"'Crash,'" he repeated, clapping me on the back. "The name feels right."

I disagreed. Recently I'd had to postpone my piloting lessons because my instructor, upon learning—in midair—who I was, became so flustered that he fainted on the instrument panel and we landed in a tree at the edge of a Walmart parking lot. Some would call that a crash, but I'm reluctant to admit it, even though in truth I was not aiming for the tree but the actual parking lot. Anyway, everybody lived, which is saying something because it was only my fourth flying lesson. Since then I've been relegated to using the sophisticated simulator in the WorldAir pilot-training complex. It was one of the perks of my on-again, off-again ownership of the airline.

Today I thanked God I got the board to hire Officer Ned as head of company security. It was a perk that turned out to benefit me, seeing as how I'd just killed one of our mechanics and was at present an official fugitive from the law. Officer Ned shook his head and handed me a peanut packet. His cellphone vibrated to life. I jumped even though the ringer was off.

"Who is it?" I whispered.

Officer Ned clicked "decline" on his screen. "LaVonda," he sighed. Then his phone dinged quietly, indicating a text message. He looked at his screen and rubbed his temples again. "She's on her way over."

"How does she know I'm here?"

"I told her I had a hunch you were hiding here," he said. Again, Officer Ned and I had a history with this airplane. I knew if I sat tight he'd figure out where I was.

A luggage tug squealed to a stop outside our hangar. I heard LaVonda calling to the policeman assigned to protect the crime scene, "I am the WorldAir Trauma Liaison, you just tell your boss that it's written in my work duties to assess all areas where trauma has occurred. And murder is damn traumatizing, you hear me? Now let me through."

It must have worked, because next we heard LaVonda scrambling up the scaffolding and onto the wing. She had one leg inside the window exit of the plane when the officer yelled at her to get down. "The murder didn't happen on the aircraft."

"Don't you be yellin' at me to get down off my own plane owned by my company I work for who gave me this important job, the duties of which . . ."

Officer Ned had had enough. He was up and through the hatch in two seconds, calling to the officer to stand down. "This is my assistant," he waved assuredly. "I've got this."

"Your *assistant*?" LaVonda lowered her voice. "You specifically said I was not your *assistant*. I like 'colleague' better. In fact, I think it's gonna say so in my . . ."

"Thank you, officer," Officer Ned said. There was some more hoarse whispering between him and LaVonda, and then I heard a strange scuttling sound come running down the aisle above me. My heart leapt. *Could it be?* I stood under the opening in the floor above me, and sure enough.

"Captain Beefheart!" I whispered excitedly. The dog jumped into my arms, licking my face, grunting and squirming like a furry little sea lion.

Captain Beefheart is a loveable mutt with a half-chewed-off ear who looked like a small crocodile covered in fur. In actuality, he's a corgi/pit bull mix (how those two breeds got together is testimony to the ingenuity of attraction). He was found as a puppy in the compactor of a trash truck after the dumpster in which he'd been abandoned was upturned inside of it. Luckily the trash man heard yelping, dug the puppy out, and dropped it off at a rescue organization. My friend Malcolm then chose Beefheart as his emotional support animal, owing to the amount of time he'd flown as an unaccompanied minor between the East Coast where his mother lived and the West Coast where his father moved to get away from her.

The thought of Malcolm made my heart sink again. I buried my face in Beefheart's neck and held back tears. Officer Ned effortlessly descended back through the hatch and then turned to help LaVonda with her attempt, which was not at all effortless.

"Get your hands off my butt." She kicked her feet and Officer Ned backed away. LaVonda perched there for a bit, half descended through the ceiling hatch, legs flailing, then finally let go and hit the floor with a thud. It's saying something about the durability of the aircraft that it didn't shake.

"Hoo! That was fun. Where's my Poochie?" She held out her arms. I held out Captain Beefheart only to have her envelop us both in her warm embrace. It was almost enough to finally make me cry. Almost. I met LaVonda Morgenstern, a former

L.A. gang member and ex-Minimart cashier, last year after I'd escaped the car trunk of an abductor—a side perk of the runaway life. LaVonda had been so good at keeping me from going into shock that I lobbied for her to come to Atlanta to serve as "Trauma Liaison" to WorldAir company security. It was a totally made-up position, but the board could not say no to me seeing as how I was a media darling and all. LaVonda now lived in Atlanta with her domestic partner and their two children.

Beefheart jumped to the floor and presented his paw to Officer Ned, who shook it firmly. This dog played a big part in foiling the hijackers of flight 1021 last year. As a result, he was a natural mascot for the airline, and since he was an emotional support canine, it made sense that he be part of the trauma-liaison team. LaVonda, in her customary manner, took their union very seriously, and considered Captain Beefheart her partner, like a police officer in the K-9 unit. Since LaVonda didn't have an office (in exchange she was assigned an iPad on a shoulder strap and a fleet of those beeping carts to maniacally drive through the concourses), she kept an elaborately padded doggie bed in a corner of Officer Ned's office, where Beefheart rested between assignments. And wherever Beefheart was, so was LaVonda. Officer Ned blustered about it, but not emphatically.

"Girl," LaVonda huffed at me. "You sure know how to get yourself into some situations. What the hell part do you play in some man getting chopped up? Tell me everything and don't leave anything out." LaVonda folded down the galley jumpseat and sat. I sat on the floor in front of her with Beefheart in my lap.

Officer Ned stood with his arms folded. "She was about to tell me when you showed up making a commotion."

"Hush," she whispered to him, then turned to me. "Now what the hell happened?"

I told them I'd been hiding here ever since the Mr. Hackman "incident" the night before, which made it kind of funny that everyone was searching for me high and wide when really I hadn't gone anywhere. A blood stain in the shape of the continent of Africa was still on the concrete below us. Last night when I peeked through the crease in the cargo door I could see the crime-scene tape crisscrossing the hangar. I imagined it made the plane look like a giant metal fly caught in a Day-Glo web. The few times I had to use the bathroom I pulled myself up through a trap door and crawled on my elbows to the lavatory in the midcabin. I made sure *not* to flush the toilet. It was an experience I wanted to repeat as little as possible.

"April, again," Officer Ned prompted me again, "how did this start?"

CHAPTER 3

It started when I crashed Uncle Otis's car yet again, during yet another DMV driving test. Ms. Washington, the DMV instructor, only agreed to give me another try because Otis had wooed her into it. I had requested another instructor, but these were clerks at the Department of Motor Vehicles; the only entertainment they got all day was when people asked for something, in which case they got to swat the request to the pavement and watch it pop. What made it worse was that Ms. Washington was now unwisely attached to my uncle Otis, and obviously figured this would be a way to ingratiate herself with him. She kept talking to me like she was going to be my new mother or something.

"April, darling, don't go crashing into a tree again, got that?" she chuckled tensely as she eased into the passenger seat.

"If I recall the news footage," a tobacco-shredded voice answered her from the backseat, "it was you who grabbed the wheel and steered it into the tree."

Ms. Washington and I both jumped nervously and turned to face Flo, who was supposed to have been waiting inside until the test was over.

"What are you doing here?" I cried.

"I figured you could use a witness, Crash." Flo lit a menthol and took a deep drag.

"Put that out immediately," Ms. Washington admonished. "I'm not about to shorten my life by breathing in your second-hand smoke."

"Why not?" Flo chuckled. "You're shortening it by getting in the car with Crash Manning here."

"If you don't put it out, I'll fail April's driving test before she puts the key in the ignition."

Flo rolled her eyes and flicked the cigarette out the window. I was very touched that she'd forgo her fifth cigarette of the morning for my sake. But sentiment aside, I also suspected Flo was here in order to recount my progress on her blog, JetHag.com, which was clocking over 20,000 unique hits a week these days. In it she divulged a slew of airline insider information that would have immediately gotten her canned but for the fact that the blog was written anonymously. I knew it was her because I recognized the stories she told and the vernacular she used, referring to passengers, coworkers, and WorldAir executives alike as "Mr. Asstard," "Miss Bitchy Pig," and "Sir Turdface." I had to admit it was entertaining reading—with the exception of her Wednesday posts, which were dedicated to the exploits of Crash Manning.

Ms. Washington buckled herself in and gripped the handle protruding from the BMW's passenger-side dashboard. "Fasten your seatbelt!" she chirped. "And be careful this time."

My seatbelt, of course, was already fastened. No disrespect to Ms. Washington, but telling me to be careful was like telling a pumpkin to be orange—it's in my nature. It's one of the reasons I hate my nickname Crash, because I am the most safety-obsessed person I know. For example, I knew that the greatest lifetime chance of crashing occurs within six months of getting a driver's license. And here was a note Otis taped to the bathroom mirror for me this morning:

TOP THREE REASONS TEENAGE DRIVERS DIE IN CAR WRECKS

1. Lack of situational awareness necessary to detect and respond to hazards
2. Miscalculating road conditions and driving too fast
3. Distraction due to something inside or outside the car

I cut my teeth on airline safety manuals, and sat rapt in my grandfather's shed as he invented half the patents that make WorldAir, as well as all airlines, a safer way to travel. My flight attendant father's death onboard an aircraft in a fire literally created a new evacuation protocol that has since saved hundreds of lives. So the last thing you need to remind me to be is careful. I didn't even bring my cellphone today for fear it would ring while I was driving.

"I never bring a cellphone with me into the car," concurred Ms. Washington. "It's like an accident magnet."

I pulled out of the parking lot without incident. I could feel Ms. Washington relax next to me. She was an attractive and tiny woman, but then I'm 5'10" so a lot of people seem short to me. Her light brown skin was dusted with freckles and she wore her mahogany-colored hair in a big bundle of dreadlocks atop her head. Flo could have related. She was barely pushing five feet and used to wear her hair in a huge bun in order to qualify for the minimum height requirement of WorldAir stewardesses back in the day.

Flo's presence actually did calm me down as I pulled into traffic and took a left on Hank Aaron Boulevard toward Memorial Avenue as Ms. Washington instructed me. Flo had been flying since 1967 and, like most old-school stews still working the skies, she was so sharp you could cut yourself just by conversing with her—so you had to be careful. I'd spent hours listening to her wax poetic about how, back in the good old days, "you could smoke in the cabin before takeoff and belt a few back with the pilots in the cockpit."

But if you ask me, those old days were not so good. The chauvinism her colleagues faced was legendary. My mother once told me that Flo, in the span of her career, had twice stood before Congress—*twice!*—as part of a petition for more fair treatment of women in the workplace.

"I'll never retire," Flo was fond of saying, "until they pry the peanuts from my cold, dead fingers."

Flo blamed herself for how my stepfather Ash turned out, seeing as how she technically gave birth to him forty-nine years ago and all. But it's not like she raised him. She popped him out in one of those Shame Compounds created throughout the Bible Belt back then for girls of ill repute who'd been knocked up and needed a way out. In 1965, Flo was hardly older than me and had aspired to be a stewardess her entire life. But those were draconian times, and no American airline would hire a woman if they knew she'd given birth (yeah, progressive, right?)—and worse, stewardesses were canned all the time for rumors to the effect they'd propagated or even gotten married on the sly. Those secret spawning wards throughout the South back then were full of stewardesses trying to keep their circumstances on the down-low so they could retain their jobs.

Ms. Washington hushed Flo when she started to sing along with Pink's "Blow Me," which was playing on the radio. I had turned left on Memorial and then veered right onto Trinity Avenue so Ms. Washington could lecture me while we drove past city hall. I was about to circle back to the DMV parking lot when my attention was drawn to a silver Rolls-Royce parked on the curb outside the corporate offices of Colgate Enterprises. That's got to be Malcolm's dad's car, I thought, and was momentarily confirmed when I caught sight of Mr. Colgate, only to realize it wasn't Malcolm's dad but Malcolm himself I was looking at.

Wow, I thought, it's funny what the last eight months have done to my best friend. When I met him he was a cherubic redhead with a warm smile and easy manner. He must have grown an inch a month since our inflight adventure last year. No longer cherubic, he was now a strapping guy, with thick wavy hair, a pronounced jawline, and green eyes that crinkled into half-moons when he smiled. I'd known him since we were 12, having spent most of that time on airplanes traveling coast to coast between divorced parents. He was the only friend I had who was my age, and the only one I knew who came close to relating to the idiocy of my custodial situation. We'd spent countless hours updating each other on the travails of our divorced parents and their ensuing custody battles. My woeful tale included a vicious adoptive father who lied and bribed his way into becoming my primary physical custodian. Astoundingly, Malcolm's story was even worse than mine. Believe me, I'd met his parents. His mother was a verbally abusive, blue-blood boozehound who reveled in using the court as a club with which to berate his father, a rich corporate mogul now disgraced and under indictment for fraud, insider trading, and tax evasion. Malcolm bounced like a pinball between them, back and forth, with them both seeming to put anger and resentment at a precedent over their son's welfare. I was amazed that Malcolm turned out to be such a kindhearted and jocular young man.

Watching Malcolm today, I had to smile. I had never seen him in a suit before, and realized I assumed I was looking at his wealthy father due in part to that and in part to the bombshell on his arm. She had platinum blonde hair, boobs big enough to be seen from outer space, and stiletto heels so high she could use them to spear lobsters.

I slowed down and waved to him, despite Ms. Washington's gentle admonishments. He didn't see me, so I attempted to toot the horn a little. The only problem was that the horn of a 1970s BMW sounded a lot like a hotel fire alarm, or maybe that was just one of my uncle Otis's upgrades to this particular BMW, but whatever the case, the sound was enough to make everyone's eardrums bleed.

Not surprisingly, everyone within a radius of two blocks jumped like nervous squirrels. Flo and I both laughed, and even Ms. Washington let a tiny smile crease the firm line of her lips. By this time, we were flush with Mr. Colgate's Rolls.

Malcolm and his paramour both jerked their heads up at the sound of the horn. I expected him to smile broadly at the sight of me, as he usually did, but instead his face froze in an odd expression. It was so unexpected that I stopped the car completely, causing the vehicles behind me to make a mild seesaw as they braked to avoid my back bumper.

"Oh, that one's gonna cost you," Ms. Washington firmly check-marked the form on her clipboard. "Another move like that, young lady . . ."

"Flo, what's wrong with Malcolm?" I interrupted.

"I don't know," Flo sounded concerned, as well.

I lowered my window and called, "Hey, Prince Charles!" I tried to sound cheery by poking mild fun at the stately condition of his attire. "What're you up to all fancy like that?"

"I, uh, I . . ." Malcolm stammered. His face turned white and his eyes were pleading. "Miss, I think you have me mistaken for someone else."

I waited for him to tell me he was kidding, and when he didn't I furrowed my brow and continued to assess the situation. That was one of the most important things you learned from the WorldAir flight attendant onboard manual—assess the situation. I couldn't believe the number of people who died like day-old fruit flies simply because they didn't bother to do this.

"Situational awareness, kid," Otis liked to point out to me with a wink. "Don't forget. Sounds simple, but it's not. You got to be aware of your surroundings." He should know, I guess. He witnessed close-hand how the lack of situational awareness can erase 583 people in the blink of an eye. In fact, I would not have been surprised if Otis had helped write the chapter on situational awareness in the WorldAir flight attendant manual. I've read the manual cover to cover a couple of times now, and the last and most important item on the checklist for situational awareness was "Use Your Intuition."

Looking at Malcolm, my intuition was screaming at me right now.

Ms. Washington urged me to continue driving, but I ignored her and focused on the scene at the side of the road. The blonde woman took care to keep her face directed away from me. It turned out she was not "on" Malcolm's arm so much as she was grabbing it and urging him into the backseat, where someone else was reaching out to pull him inside. Malcolm was still staring at me in a white-faced panic as the woman placed her hand on the top of his head while she and the man both pulled and shoved him into the car. *What the hell?* The man in the backseat then urged the driver to go, and it was then that I recognized Mr. Hackman.

"That bastard!" Flo hissed from behind me.

The sight of Mr. Hackman brought out anger in me, as well. He was a small, paunch-bellied, balding man who looked older than his 52 years. He had successfully lobbied against unionization of the WorldAir mechanics, only to appoint himself official corporate liaison solely for the purpose of conceding the new contract in obvious favor of management. We figured he did this in order to accept heavy bribes, a contention that was backed up by the McMansion he acquired in Alpharetta soon afterward. By then Molly told us she had left him, due to the spousal abuse as well as the apartment she discovered he kept downtown across the street from the Cheetah so he could house a small harem of strippers at his beck and call. But evidently he didn't want Molly to go on her own terms. So he ambushed her in the garage one night, and beat her with a lawnmower blade until her head was hardly more than pulp.

Today the case was "pending," as the police put it, and was on the verge of going cold because the only witness, Molly herself, was on life support and couldn't finger her attacker. My friend Alby, a former flight attendant who now ran her own small law practice, is the sole reason Molly still breathes. The minute the police declined to charge him, Mr. Hackman was at the hospital as Molly's next of kin demanding the removal of her life support. I happened to be in her room at the time, delivering my daily bouquet, when suddenly Mr. Hackman barreled in with a gaggle of nurses, insisting she be unplugged because "it's what she would have wanted."

Panicked, I got Alby on the phone, and she was able to petition for emergency custody of Molly and thus put off any unplugging for at least ten days, at which point Mr. Hackman would have to appear in court to argue against the petition. Mr. Hackman was livid, and he'd been beaming heavy hate vibes at me ever since. Officer Ned called some old contacts at the station and found out that Mr. Hackman had taken out a half-million-dollar life-insurance policy on Molly, and Alby and I were the only things keeping him from collecting it right away.

So the sight of Mr. Hackman usually frightened and angered me, but now here he was rough-handling my friend Malcolm, which especially got my blood to boiling. I yanked the parking brake and lay on the horn with both hands. Pedestrians covered their ears and stared at me. Ms. Washington hooted with consternation and told me to keep driving. Flo encouraged me from the backseat. "Block 'em in, kid!"

Mr. Hackman flailed furiously at the driver, urging him forward. The driver looked over his shoulder at us and I felt my blood turn to ice.

"Ash, you bastard!" I screamed.

"Call me Dad," he sneered back at me. He put the Rolls in gear, slammed on the gas, and basically shoved us out of the way with barely a dent in the expensive Rolls bumper.

We, on the other hand, didn't fare so well. The front bumper of our BMW, probably in place with nothing but staples anyway, peeled halfway off and hung to the ground like a limp banana leaf. "They're getting away!" Flo harped, tossing another cigarette out the window.

I disengaged the parking brake, shoved the transmission in gear, and left skid marks smoking on the asphalt as I tore off after them. It soon became evident that, while Otis may not have cared a single bit about the outward appearance of this car, he certainly turbocharged the engine. We shot out like a rocket and caught up to them instantly. By this point Ms. Washington had slipped into such a state of panic that all she seemed able to do was clutch the dashboard handle, her eyes bulging and her body stiff with fear. And no wonder: Ash had begun bumping us with the Rolls in an effort to push us off the road or into oncoming traffic. At one point it was like we were hitched together as we turned left onto Central Avenue. A block later we would empty into the freeway. *The freeway.* I had never driven on the freeway.

"Looks like we have company," Flo said. I glanced up to see the police cars in the rearview mirror, then I heard their sirens. Ash yanked the Rolls to the right and broke away from us, taking Ms. Washington's door with him. The door fell to the ground in a flurry of sparks and cartwheeled along the freeway before crashing into the windshield of one of the police cars in our pursuit. *Oh, Christ,* I winced, *I hope the officer is okay.* Next to me, Ms. Washington was pale against her freckles. The open road whizzed by at her side, and she had begun to hyperventilate.

The engine of the Rolls-Royce is a wonder of mechanical construction. In fact, it can be found in many of the jet casings of the aircraft that compose the fleet of WorldAir. But it was nothing compared to the bionic power of whatever Otis had put under the hood of his jalopy of an old BMW, because not only were we able to outrun the police, we were also able to match the Rolls in speed and maneuverability in spite of the extra wind drag created by our missing door.

"Woo hoo!" Flo kept hollering from the backseat, until Mr. Hackman rolled down his window and fired a gun at us.

"Heads down! Stay low!" I screamed out of habit from memorizing the flight attendant crash commands in my mother's onboard manual. Ms. Washington had already lowered her head down to her arms, and I would have thought she'd fainted but for her constant keening, "Oh, Lord Christ on the Cross! Jesus God in the Glory of Heaven! Deliver us from this evil! Deliver us!"

I could smell smoke, but if Mr. Hackman had hit our engine, the BMW didn't betray it. I kept in close pursuit until our cars gained on a Volvo station wagon filled with a young family. Two kids were in the extra third-row seat that faced away from the driver, toward us. Mr. Hackman thrust his gun out the window, not at us, but at them, making it clear he intended to fire at their car if we kept chasing him.

"April," Flo's voice was calm. "Back off." I took my foot off the gas and kept my eyes on Malcolm, who had turned back to face me as the Rolls disappeared into the distance.

But there was no time for tears. Suddenly the engine sounded like a blender full of bolts, so I pulled to the emergency lane and came to a stop. Once we were stopped the source of the smoke smell became evident, as black clouds began billowing from beneath our hood. Flo and I quickly got out of the car and had to extricate poor wide-eyed Ms. Washington, who was stiff and still praying. Seconds later the BMW burst into flames as high as a four-story building. *Dammit.* I heard the sirens as the remaining officers caught up with us, as well as the sound of something else. What was that?

I shaded my eyes and looked up. *Helicopters!* Double dammit. One for the police and one for the news. Then my curses were drowned out by the explosion.

Otis's car blew up like a bomb. And if I thought the flames were high before, they were nothing compared to now. Luckily we three had reached a safe distance away, but I wish I could say the same for the news copter. A piece of shrapnel hit the helicopter windshield, which so panicked the pilot that he put the thing down right smack on the freeway. The pilot discerned too late that he planted the machine too close to the burning car, but luckily he was able to jump out and run away before his helicopter burst into flames as well.

By this time traffic was stopped for miles in each direction. The heat, the flames, the flashing sirens—the catastrophe was almost hypnotizing. I heard a man chuckle near me. "This is great. This is amazing." I turned to see Clay Roundtree standing next to me with his pen poised above a notebook.

"Oh, my God!" I cried. "How did you get here?"

Flo stepped between us. "Relax, Crash," she said. "I texted him when we left the DMV. He's been behind us the whole time." I was speechless. My eyes yanked furiously back and forth between them. I was just about to scream when suddenly we were surrounded by officers with their guns drawn.

"Who is the driver of this vehicle," one shouted angrily. Flo and Mr. Roundtree backed away from me slowly, as did

Ms. Washington. Slowly, I raised my hands above my head and tried to look meek. "I don't have my license yet."

As the officer turned me around to cuff me, I was briefly blinded by the flash from an iPhone camera. "Amazing," Mr. Roundtree chuckled as I was shoved into the back of a squad car.

CHAPTER 4

What happened next is why I seriously worry about the state of the Atlanta police department sometimes. In particular their quality of training. First, the officer who cuffed me neglected to thoroughly tighten the brace around my right wrist. So I waited until I was locked inside the police car to easily slip my hand out of it. From there I simply waited patiently, or as patiently as I could given that I'd just witnessed the kidnapping of my best friend along with the complete collapse of civil order along an eight-mile stretch of freeway.

Tow trucks and emergency vehicles had finally arrived. The burning BMW and helicopter had been doused by a fire truck that pulled up on the other side of the freeway divider. Once the fire was out the smoke thickened like soup. For a bit. And so many emergency lights were flashing it looked like an outdoor disco. The traffic was so gridlocked that people had given up any thought of getting to their destinations and gotten out of their cars to commune together, take photos, and comment on the sight.

Eyes were everywhere but on me, for once. So I took this opportunity to, yes, *assess my situation.* First I noticed that the officer had left the car running, I assumed in order to maintain climate control on this cold night. On top of that, the thick Plexiglas security partition—the one that separated the front and backseats of the police vehicle—had been kindly left lowered a few inches in order for some of that heat to pass through to the backseat, probably to avoid lawsuits from suspects freezing to death on the way to being booked.

I could see how these circumstances would be useless to someone with her hands cuffed behind her back. But thankfully my hands were free because the police officer was nice enough to consider my comfort when cuffing me. I took a stealthy look around to assure that everyone was still looking at the spectacle on the freeway instead of at me, and was pleased to see that people had begun returning to their cars at the urging of the officers, who were all involved in directing traffic, which had begun to move again at the pace of sludge.

I'm skinny. There, I said it. I have arms like broomsticks. In fact, some of the tabloids had taken to insisting people should be worried about my weight. I'm sure this was in retaliation against all the other tabloids that were touting me as a "winsome beauty." Everything comes full circle in the media, believe me. I was sure if I gained five pounds I'd be labeled porky or even pregnant, so the last thing on my list of concerns was my image. Obviously, because this right here was my fourth public wreck.

Anyway, with my skinny arms and that two-inch opening, it was almost effortless to reach through the lowered partition to the driver-side door handle and press the button to lower one of the power windows in the backseat of the police car. From there I slipped through the window to the ground. Crouching, I waddled from car to stranded car, jiggling door handles until one opened. It was one of those ridiculous big black Humvees that probably ran on the blood of endangered white rhinos or something. The tractor wheels practically came up to my waist. I could hear the ozone weeping as I crept inside to lay on the floorboard of the backseat.

I was not a second too soon. Almost immediately the driver returned and got behind the wheel, then a passenger entered on the other side and both doors slammed with a comforting *thunk*. The engine revved reliably and I felt us begin to creep along with the rest of the directed traffic. I heard the flicking of a butane lighter, then the unmistakable smell of menthol cigarette smoke.

Flo! I thought excitedly.

"Uh, do you mind not smoking in my car?" I heard Mr. Roundtree say. I glowered from my hiding place.

"Your car doesn't need my cigarette to smell like smoke," Flo said, lowering her window, which allowed the burning smell from outside to make her point.

"Don't just toss it outside! There's probably still fuel spilled on the road!"

"Well, what the hell do you want me to do with it then?" Flo inhaled deeply, obviously trying to get in as many hits as possible before being forced to relinquish her cigarette. "There ain't exactly an ashtray in here."

"Just . . ." He sighed in exasperation. "Okay, keep it until we get past the police, then throw it out."

"At this pace I'll have to light another one," Flo chuckled.

Mr. Roundtree laughed nervously. "I guess we're lucky no one got killed. No one got killed, right?"

"Hell if I know."

"What's this now?" he grumbled. "A road block?"

I crawled into the backseat and sat upright. It was dark out and Flo and Mr. Roundtree were focused forward and still hadn't noticed me. I figured if there was a roadblock it'd be a lot less conspicuous if I were sitting out in the open like any number of other innocent passengers. I doubt that the officers had the time to be super detailed when they were checking every car for escaped detainees, so at this point they were probably looking for anything suspicious, and nothing is more suspicious-looking than a teenager hiding on the floorboard behind the driver's seat. I made sure to tuck my cuffed hand out of sight.

Our car crawled toward an officer shining his flashlight into the cars before directing them to move on. When we reached him, Mr. Roundtree rolled down his window and asked, "Is there a problem, officer?"

"None that you need to worry about," he answered. Then his flashlight settled on me in the backseat. "Who's that?"

They all craned their necks in my direction. Mr. Roundtree was so startled it looked like someone touched him with the hot end of an electrical cable. Flo, on the other hand, simply smiled broadly and said, "Why, that's my granddaughter. My son and I are taking her to Disney World, that is if we can catch our flight."

The officer shined his light on Mr. Roundtree. "This is your daughter?"

His head nodded with slow trepidation. "Uh, we came from Alpharetta . . ."

"Your plates read Forsyth County, which is way south of Alpharetta," the officer noted suspiciously.

"What he means is we had to pick her up at her mother's," Flo interrupted. "They live in Alpharetta and her mother couldn't be bothered to take her to the airport to meet us."

The officer lowered his flashlight and said, "I know what that's like. Hope you make your flight."

"Thanks, officer!" Flo called out as Mr. Roundtree raised the window and hit the gas.

"Oh my God oh my God oh my God . . ." he keened. "I'm abetting an escaped convict! Whadoo I do? Whadoo I do?"

"I'm not a *convict*," I said. "I haven't been *convicted* of anything."

"Calm down," Flo told Mr. Roundtree. Then she turned to me, her face alight. "Good job, Crash! How'd you know which car to get into?"

"I didn't. I just opened the first unlocked door and got inside."

Just then we saw Ms. Washington ambling along the side of the freeway, looking dazed. Traffic was still moving slowly enough for us to stop and call to her from the second lane without causing too many people to honk and curse at us. "Do you need a ride?" I asked her. My voice seemed to startle her. She looked up and then away, shaking her head fervently.

"I think she's in shock or something," I told Flo.

"No shit."

We couldn't just leave her to wander the freeway, traumatized, I thought. "Please, Ms. Washington, get in the car. Look, I'm not the one driving. See? I'm in the backseat."

At Flo's urging, Roundtree used his urban tank to muscle the other cars out of the way so we could be next to Ms. Washington. It was the surrounding horn-honking more than anything that finally got her to acquiesce and get in the backseat with me. As a driving instructor, it must have affected her sense of roadway decorum for us to be hindering traffic flow while haranguing her to come inside the car. It must have been stronger even than her sense of personal safety, because it was obvious she felt more out of harm's way wandering the concrete embankment on the freeway than she did inside a car with me. She settled herself next to me and buckled herself in with a huff. Flo introduced her to Roundtree, who decorously declared his pleasure to make her acquaintance, which she ignored.

"What's that?" she indicated my left wrist.

"Handcuff," I lifted it to show her the dangling end.

Mr. Roundtree laughed a bit hysterically. "Yeah, you're not a convict."

"Do you have a paper clip?" I asked her.

"Safety pin do?" she sighed.

"Sure."

Handcuffs were the easiest locks to pick, if you asked me. In most cases, all you had to do was insert a small, stiff wire along the top of the tooth-and-cog wrist brace where the ratcheted lever connected to the brace. The wire held the locking tooth up and away from the ratchet. It took me less than a minute to pick the lock and release my remaining wrist from the restraint. I slipped the handcuffs into my back pocket, where I realized I'd put the set of picks Otis had given me and mentally slapped my forehead. I specifically carried them there in case I ever did get handcuffed. But I always envisioned it happening by an abductor, not a lawman.

I don't carry a backpack anymore, but my usual uniform included a pair of cargo pants and a zip-up sweatshirt, an ensemble with enough pockets to tote the contents of an entire toolbox if I wanted. I put the safety pin in a pocket along my thigh and felt the presence of a nine-volt battery I'd slipped in there the other day after Otis left it on the kitchen table. Like him, I found it hard to throw away useful things. Sometimes I even forgot all the stuff I was carrying.

"So, where're we headed?" Flo asked me.

"Hackman's place," I answered.

"What?" hollered Roundtree. "Who is Hackman? And why are we not going to the police to turn you in?"

"Turn me in for what?"

"Escaping police custody for one," Roundtree ran his fingers worriedly through his thinning red hair. It was a feature that made it easy for me to spot him in a media horde. Few reporters have quite the freckled scalp and copper-colored comb-over that Roundtree sported. Add his penchant for white suits, goatees, and neon Fluevog shoes and you have a guy who could stealthily blend into any crowd of clownfish on the face of the earth. But since clownfish aren't common in the streets of Atlanta, Roundtree sticks out like a disco ball in a bucket of rusty crowbars.

"So, Scooter, now you want to implicate yourself in abetting the escape of a suspected criminal?" Flo intervened. (By the way, she called all skinny guys "Scooter.")

"I wouldn't be implicating myself if I just drove to the police station right now to turn her in."

"Where's the story in that?" Flo reminded him.

"Believe me," Roundtree responded, "I have plenty of material. I don't need to jeopardize my journalistic ethics."

"What ethics? You write a blog."

Suddenly I understood how these two were in cahoots. Roundtree must have been sending web traffic to her blog in exchange for information and vice versa. This would explain Flo's explosion in cyber popularity over the last year, given that the *Southern Times* was a major metropolitan newspaper that had survived extinction by booting most of their trained writers in favor of bloggers, "citizen journalists" (I'm sorry, I can never say that phrase without the air quotes around it), and entertainment writers like Roundtree (I feel air quotes are in order for the word "entertainment" here, as well), who are a hybrid of the two. (His byline reads, "I write about trending topics.") I felt betrayed by how Flo apparently sold me out as click bait for her website, and I resolved to chew her up for it later.

"We're going to the police right now," Roundtree added, although the car continued to creep along at the pace of a glacier, softening the impact of his declaration.

"When you say 'material' you mean photos, right?" Flo asked. "Because I have your iPhone right here." She held it up and tossed it to me before Roundtree could snatch it back from her. I quickly began flipping through his recent photographs and was frustrated to see he'd started snapping pictures from as early as my arrival at the DMV for my driving test that afternoon.

"Give that back!" Roundtree insisted, flailing his right arm behind him in a blind sweep while he kept his eye on the road to steady his driving. Ms. Washington seemed to be impressed with his priorities.

"Don't give it back," Flo instructed me, then turned back to him. "Now, Scooter, we are not nearly done with the day's adventure. If you want to drop us off you can, but you'll have to live without your pictures until we're sure you haven't ratted us out to the police."

"Keep it. I don't need the iPhone," Roundtree huffed. "Everything instantly uploads to my iCloud account. I can access it anytime I want from anywhere."

"Who do you think you're dealing with, some farty old shut-in?" Flo countered. I chuckled in spite of myself. "I sent the pictures to my account and then deleted them from your Photo Stream. You really should implement a lock on your iPhone."

The fact that I was flipping through Roundtree's recent photos showed that Flo was lying when she said she'd deleted them, but he must have believed they were gone because he banged his steering wheel and let loose an expletive. I continued to flip through the pictures and decided not to delete them all because the stream was a pretty good representation of what had happened since we left the parking lot of the DMV. Here was the proof to show I was trying to stop a crime in case I ever did get hauled into the hoosegow. He got a few of Hackman aiming a gun at us and even snapped a number of angles of Malcolm before he was shoved into the car. It's probably a miracle Roundtree didn't get in an accident himself. Otis and Ms. Washington both would have scolded him for being distracted by incidents outside the vehicle. I selected all the photos and emailed them to myself so I could retrieve them on the iPad mini I kept in Officer Ned's office. Speaking of, I used the phone to call him, but he probably didn't pick up because he didn't recognize the number. Then I left a message telling him what really happened, because no doubt he would have gotten the media version by now.

We were halfway to Alpharetta before I remembered that Ms. Washington needed to be taken home. "Wait, we should drop you off," I told her. "Where do you live?"

"College Park," she replied.

"We just drove a half hour in the opposite direction, why didn't you say anything?"

She shrugged and straightened her tortoise-shell eyeglasses. "My kids are grown. My cat is fed. Ain't nobody anxious for me to get home." She fiddled with the handles of her embroidered Guatemalan handbag. "I saw that boy get taken. He must be scared."

Flo and I both assessed her with skepticism. For my part, I didn't doubt her intent—after listening to our conversation she seemed to want to help. I was just skeptical about how helpful she could be. She practically lapsed into catatonia during a simple car chase. Granted, bullets were flying and our car was kind of disintegrating around us, but still. Focus.

"I don't know," Flo intoned. "Maybe we can drop her off at the next gas station."

"She's not a stray dog!" I admonished Flo, who shrugged and lit another cigarette to the consternation of Roundtree. She cracked the window to hold the lit end outside, but the wind caught it and it flew from her hand.

"Dammit." She produced a stick of gum from her purse and popped it in her mouth.

Ms. Washington straightened in her seat. "I work at the DMV. I spend most of my time in a windowless room behind three inches of Plexiglas. Before today the most exciting thing that ever happened at work was when we ran out of decaf. We make the rules, we follow the rules, we enforce the rules. But aside from the rules, there is right and wrong. And I saw that boy get taken. That's wrong."

"Why don't you want us to go to the police?" I asked, knowing that my call to Officer Ned, in my opinion, was just as good if not better.

She shrugged again. "I know how the city works. The first thing they're gonna do is arrest all of us, then wait for an arraignment date to sort things out. Do you have time for that?" She waited for a response, which there was none. "I didn't think so."

"Fine, she's coming with us," Roundtree interjected. "Where am I going?"

I instructed him to take Windward Parkway, turn right, then left, then look for the most obnoxious new-built mega home on the street. The concrete roaring phoenix statues sitting sentry at the fence entry were a dead giveaway. There wasn't actually a gate, mind you, just giant fence posts. I bet he built them just for the statues. We drove to the front door via a circular driveway lined with expensive polished pea gravel. The house itself was a myriad of aimless gray stucco gables and bay windows that I'm sure would have made any Pillsbury recipe winner pee in her pants with joy, but personally I'd rather live under a freeway overpass than this cheaply built suburban-developer white elephant. A camping tent probably had better bones than this thing.

"I'm not having any part of breaking and entering," Roundtree announced.

"Who's breaking anything?" Flo asked. "Crash here has a key." She meant the set of lock picks given to me by Otis.

"I'll wait for you down the street." Roundtree stuck out his palm. "I'll need my phone."

"Take mine," Flo tossed him her Galaxy and he wrinkled his nose like she'd handed him a turd. "And take her, too," Flo indicated Ms. Washington, who didn't object. "We'll text you when we want you to come get us."

"I'll make sure he doesn't leave you behind," Ms. Washington offered. I cracked a half smile, wondering just what she could do to stop him. Anyway, I was pretty certain Roundtree wouldn't pass up a chance for an exclusive on this story, as his entire beat at the newspaper consisted solely of me, "a trending topic," it seemed. Roundtree pulled away from the house with his lights out, leaving me and Flo to approach the front door.

"What's that smell?" I asked.

"It's Hackman's place. He probably has a basement full of dead hookers," Flo said. Lovely.

The first thing we noticed when we entered the foyer, aside from the smell, was the incessant barking coming from the hall closet. Flo opened the door and tiny white ball of fluff flew into her arms. "That bastard! He locked the dog in the closet!"

"Is that a dog?"

I wouldn't have believed it if I didn't hear it bark. It was the smallest dog I'd ever seen, no bigger than a bird. It must have been part Pomeranian, part miniature Chihuahua, and part guinea pig. It nuzzled into Flo's neck and would have seamlessly blended with her short-cropped white hair if not for its tail stub, which wagged like a hummingbird wing above a perfect rosebud of a dog butt.

"Molly just got her before she went into the hospital, didn't she, little sweetie peetie pucker butt?" Flo showered the dog's teacup face with kisses. I'd never seen Flo be so affectionate. The dog was getting the kind of lip action normally reserved for her cigarettes.

"What's its name?"

"Fifi Trixibelle II, after my fourth husband's sweet pit bull. I suggested it to Molly and she liked it, didn't she?" Flo cooed to the dog.

"I guess this explains the smell," I surmised, pointing to the bottom of the closet, which was mottled with animal waste. What a prick that Hackman was.

"The only reason he keeps Trixi alive is because of the insurance policy, which keeps him from liquidating any assets while the settlement is in escrow," Flo explained. "Alby made sure the dog was listed as an asset." I was certain Hackman planned to whack the dog the minute Molly flatlined, so we couldn't leave it there. Flo held onto her as we made our way through the house. Odd, but the smell got worse as we got farther from the closet.

In contrast to its opulent exterior, the inside of the house was a squalid sty. Hackman appeared to live like a bear with furniture, and what furniture there was looked left over from a frat-house fire sale. Cigarette burns covered the chunky chuck-wagon sofa set as well as the upended decoupage coffee and end tables. The only adornment on the walls appeared to be food stains. A lot of food stains. Cardboard pizza containers littered the carpet along with candy bar wrappers, beer cans, empty potato chip bags, and overflowing ashtrays. The food containers all looked partially shredded, as did a pile of mail that lay on the other side of the front door directly under the mail slot. Something glinted among the debris on the carpet and I bent to pick it up. My blood turned cold.

"What's that?" Flo asked.

"Malcolm's medical-alert bracelet. He's allergic to penicillin." I put it in my pocket and straightened to take in the scene. "What the hell happened here?" I asked. "Does it normally look like this?

"Uh, hard to say," Flo ventured. "He's such a slob."

The kitchen was worse. Grease splattered on the walls, dirty plates piled on every surface, trash everywhere except for inside the trash bin. There was zero dog food to be seen, and it occurred to me with horror that Trixi must have been subsisting on whatever discarded scraps she could forage. That would explain the shredded pizza boxes and even the torn-up mail, as dogs often like to eat envelopes because of the flavored adhesive on the other side of the flaps.

"What are we looking for?" asked Flo. Anything that looks out of the ordinary, I told her. "Does any of this look ordinary?" she said, and I saw her point. On the kitchen counter next to the wall phone, I spotted a long strip of adhesive backing, blank but for a baggage claim sticker on the end. "ATL-GCM" the ticket read, indicating a flight to Grand Cayman that left at 9:32 the next evening. I pocketed it, along with the small notepad next to it. Trixi whimpered from Flo's arms as we circled back to explore the rest of the layout.

How did they get food on the hallway walls? I wondered. It looked like Hackman and his buddies had covered themselves in ketchup and held a freestyle wrestling match all over the house. The downstairs hallway was illuminated by a light coming from the bath off the master bedroom. Instinctively we walked toward it, following the streaks on the walls. Looking back I'm amazed at how the human brain is capable of blocking out the obvious when the obvious is too terrible to conceive. Even I, a person who was no stranger to the awfulness that people are capable of inflicting on each other, a person who prides herself on extensive self-imposed training for emergency situations—jaded as I was, I could not see the writing on the literal walls.

Flo got to the bathroom before I did. I noticed that, curiously, on the bathroom doorjamb there was one of those lift locks like you see on the interior of hotel rooms to fortify the door from intruders. Only this lift lock was on the exterior of the door. Flo pulled the door fully open, stepped back, turned around, and tried to keep me from going inside. But it was no use. I could see a panoramic reflection in the mirror over the sink. The blood-streaked mirror. I could see the body face-down in the bathtub, the bits of brain and bone that splattered the tile above it.

"Malcolm!" I screamed.

CHAPTER 5

Flo tried to hold me back, but I begged her to let me go and she did. She turned to text Roundtree to make an urgent plea that he come back to get us ASAP. I ran to the tub and stopped short of touching the body. There was no doubt he was dead. The entire back of his head was missing. I tried to calm myself. It took all of my resolve. His suit jacket hung on a towel hook. In the sink there was a collection of kitchen knives that appeared to have been hastily rinsed, along with a long cable that looked like it had been cut from a vacuum cleaner. I counted 26 stab wounds through his tailored peach-colored dress shirt, as well as ligature marks on his wrists and neck. One arm draped over the edge of the tub showed that his left hand had three of the five fingernails pulled out. My mind went wild then.

He was right there, I practically could have touched him from my car window right there on the curb before they shoved him into the car. I actually created the traffic jam that gave them the time to come here ahead of us and do this. I covered my mouth and sobbed.

Stop, a voice inside me said. *April, stop and assess the situation.*

It wasn't my voice, I don't know where it came from, but believe me, it had an immediate effect. I stopped sobbing and called to Flo to bring me Roundtree's iPhone. She hung up and with much trepidation entered the bathroom to hand me the phone. Trixibelle turned her head away over Flo's shoulder as if to bleach the image of the scene from her mind. I flipped through Roundtree's photographs until I got to those that showed Malcolm during his abduction. I zoomed in to get a closer look at the collar peeking out from the top of his Brooks Brothers suit.

"What color is that?" I asked Flo. I wanted to make sure there was good reason before I upset a crime scene.

"I dunno, kid," Flo said wearily, her eyes trying to find a place to fix that wasn't appalling. Finally she settled on closing them all together. "Please let's get out of here."

I peered intently at the photo. In it, Malcolm's shirt looked to be baby blue with pin stripes. I slipped the iPhone into one of my pockets. "Help me turn him over."

"April, I . . . c'mon," Flo implored, but then used her boot-clad foot to help me push on the body's shoulder until it lay face up in the tub.

One eye remained in his skull and the other hung by a string of nerves and rested inside his gaping mouth. As horrifying as this was, I sat back and felt the relief wash over me like the effect of a strong drug. These eyes did not belong to my friend Malcolm, but his father Morton Colgate. To further substantiate this discovery, the corpse's gaping mouth showed gold fillings. Most of his scalp was missing, but the remainder retained wisps of thick gray hair.

"Oh, thank God," Flo placed her hand on my shoulder. I could feel her shaking with relief. "Thank God, thank God, thank God." I stood to hug Flo, both of us crying in relief. I knew Malcolm's dad had been under investigation for tax evasion since 2010, but wondered what he could have done to deserve such a fate. I knew his ex-wife, Malcolm's mom, had a hatred for him that could compare with the heat of a hundred suns, but to torture and mutilate him like this? I had a hard time believing it. Someone had been trying to get him to talk. I wondered if he told them what they wanted to hear.

Trixibelle whined loudly. "Look, Trixi's crying, too," Flo said.

That might have been true, but she wasn't crying about the same thing we were. I pulled away from Flo. "Do you smell gasoline?" Before she could answer I caught the reflection of movement in the mirror above the sink. Suddenly Hackman's portly physique filled the doorway.

He pointed a gun at Flo's face. "Gimme the dog."

CHAPTER 6

Here's the thing about guns: people generally think you have to freeze when someone points one at you. I never understood this, because it would be way easier to hit a frozen target than a moving one. Flo and I are very much on the same page about this, having been shot at a number of times in the recent past. Otis is of the same sentiment. Here is his entire list on what to do when someone has a gun at your head:

WHAT TO DO WHEN SOMEONE HAS A GUN AT YOUR HEAD

1. **Attack Without Hesitation.** Hesitation will get you killed. In a fight for your life you must be prepared to attack back *without hesitation.*

I swatted the gun out of Hackman's hand in the same instance that Flo's boot-clad foot found solid purchase in a vicious kick to his crotch. The gun discharged and shattered the mirror before landing in the sink on top of the pile of cable and knives. Hackman screamed, doubled over, then quickly dove for the gun at the same time I did. Flo, still holding Trixi, continued to kick at him furiously. He got to the gun before me, but barely. "Goddammit!" he growled, as I swatted it away again, but not before another wild shot rang out that this time, horribly, ricocheted off the tile, and hit Mr. Colgate in the neck. The gun scuttled into the toilet with a loud splash.

I shut the lid and sat on it. Hackman next grabbed one of the knives on the floor, but Flo already had one from the sink. She stepped on his wrist, breaking the blade from the handle, and slashed his upper arm. He jumped up howling and stumbled back into the bedroom. Flo closed the bathroom door and locked it from inside. She leaned against the vanity gasping for air. Through the whole ordeal, she never loosened her grip on the dog.

"I'm impressed," I said when we got a chance to breathe.

"Kicking mean old redneck ass is my catnip."

The smell of gasoline wafted strongly again. I could hear Hackman sloshing it on the carpet outside the bathroom door. "Bitches!" he shouted. We heard footsteps run up the stairway.

"What are you *doing*?" I heard Ash call after him. I never thought I'd be so happy to hear his voice. Of all the awful things he'd done in the past, I never thought of Ash as an actual murderer. Mean, yes. Idiotic, yes. Selfish, yes—I could have gone on with the litany of characteristics that led to my low opinion of the man, starting with the fact that, 12 years ago, he moved in on my bereft, recently widowed mother like a hyena on the hunt. Even today he remained handsome in an oily, soap-opera-actor kind of way, with wavy blond hair and a jawline like it was carved out of marble. I could almost see why women flocked to him like horseflies to a horse turd, but for me personally it would be hard to get past the vapid black hole he has for a soul. But no disrespect to those who fell for his act. I've known the man since I was four. I was there at the front line while he was out to take my mother for everything she had, then zeroed in on the thing that mattered most to her: me. Through bribes, lies, and the simple idiocy of the Atlanta Fulton County family court system, Ash finagled himself into being declared my primary physical custodian. Later I learned it was due to an inheritance I had coming, and how, as my parental custodian, he was in line to be the executor of all the money. It was a clever plan, but it interfered with bigger issues at the time, such as those of the WorldAir CEO, who colluded to bomb one of his company's own airplanes in order to keep my grandfather's patent rights under wraps.

So, yeah, Ash may have been a selfish heartless narcissist, a greedy mean-spirited spineless sea urchin of a man, but he wasn't a killer. Surely he wouldn't stand by and allow his stepdaughter—let alone his biological mother—be burned alive in a windowless bathroom alongside the desecrated corpse of a torture victim. Right?

"Don't kill the dog! We need the dog!" Ash shouted. The dog? *That bastard.*

"We don't need the dog *alive*," Hackman shouted back. "Once this place burns down we can come back and dig through the rubble and dig it out. I'll get another one just like it to show the insurance adjuster."

"Where's the claim ticket?"

"I thought you had it!" Hackman yelled angrily.

"What the hell?" Flo said, clutching the dog close to her. I could see the anger in her eyes. Perhaps she knew Ash better even than I did. "Ash Manning," she shouted through the door, "don't you dare burn us down."

Ash either ignored her or didn't hear her, because in that instant, in a loud *whoosh!,* I heard the bedroom ignite in a furious blaze. Oh, Christ, really? How cliché, burning the evidence of a crime scene. I should have known Ash would show zero imagination. I looked around the bathroom to see if there was anything I could use to help us escape.

"We gotta get outta here," Flo unlocked our door and tried to push it open, only to find that Hackman had lowered the flip lock on the other side. I wasn't surprised. Obviously this was why the lock was there in the first place, to keep Mr. Colgate locked inside while they held him hostage. How convenient it must have been for Hackman to use it on us. My blood boiled at the thought of him, all smug thinking he'd won one over on us. Flo kicked at the door furiously to no avail. It was solid wood, either a fluke of design for such a cheaply built house or, more chilling, a deliberate reinforcement for the purpose of its recent use. I extracted the handgun from the toilet and futilely tried to fire it against the door. The gun would be useless until the cartridges fully dried, so I put it in my pocket.

"Well, what the hell would MacGyver do?" Flo mused.

It was a legitimate question. Flo and I were both devoted fans of the old *MacGyver* TV series. We'd seen each episode at least four times, and some of our favorites up to ten. It had been our routine to watch two episodes each Wednesday night on Netflix, then quiz each other afterward. Flo in particular had an obsession that bordered on rabid. Long ago she'd tattooed "MacGyver" on her hip, and just this year she bought the actual houseboat that had been used as his home in the television series.

She found it on eBay for just $36,000. Right now it's docked at Grant's Landing in Vancouver and uninhabitable, but it's fun to go up there with her every few months or so to help her make repairs in the hopes that one day she may retire there, despite Flo's adamant proclamation that she'll retire when she's dead.

At the thought of Flo dead, I shot into action, quickly rifling through the contents of the medicine cabinet, then looking under the sink. All I could find was four rolls of toilet paper, a 1981 issue of *Playboy* magazine, and a small container of dental floss. Perfect, I thought. I lifted the lid of the toilet and I tossed each roll of toilet paper into the water in order to quickly soak them through. Sodden rolls of toilet paper actually shrink in size but vastly increase in density, so the four of them end-to-end created a nice wet plug in order to keep the smoke and fire from seeping in from under the door. I left an opening about four inches wide directly under the doorknob, then ripped the cover from the magazine and slipped it through so it lay flat on the floor and flush next to the doorjamb, praying that the flames wouldn't reach it.

Next I retrieved the knife blade that had broken from its handle when Flo stepped on Hackman's hand earlier. It was a small paring blade, and I allowed myself a single cringe thinking about the agony it must have inflicted on poor Mr. Colgate, then I tied the blade to the end of the dental floss, anchoring the knot around a hole at its base, and slipped it through the crack at the top of the door.

Since this was an interior door there was no insulated stripping along the jamb, and the blade slipped through to the other side easily. I lowered it until I could feel it touch the magazine cover at the bottom. Luckily there was enough floss to traverse the length of the door as well as allow me to keep ahold of it from the other side.

"Flo, can you—gently—pull the magazine cover with the blade on top of it back inside the bathroom?" I directed her. She knew what I was aiming for; the blade served as a weight so we could loop the dental floss out and around the door. She did as I asked, then handed me the magazine cover with the small blade tucked between the breasts of the puffy-haired cover model.

"I think I know her," Flo's chuckle ended in a cough. The smoke was getting so thick it was starting to turn the room gray. The door, too, was getting hot. Flo twisted the doorknob in order to keep the tongue from blocking the string, and I wrapped each end of the floss around my hands and jostled the ends up and down the side crack of the doorjamb until I could feel it encounter the flip lock on the other side. A flip lock is only effective because of the tension created when the metal flap is in its down, or locked, position flat against the door. To unlock it you simply have to lift the metal flap to release the tension in its hinges; this allows the metal flap to turn parallel to the doorjamb, leaving the door free to open.

"Here goes nothing," I said, and yanked up on the thin loop of twine. We heard the flip lock pop up from its hinges and Flo threw open the door.

The conditions were dire. The only area not engulfed in flames was the bathroom where we were standing. I ran back inside, grabbed the handheld shower nozzle, and cranked the water full blast. Flo had taken Mr. Colgate's jacket from the towel rack and wrapped it around Trixi, holding the shaking bundle under her arm.

"What are we going to do?" she shouted before covering her mouth with the crook of her arm. My mind spun like a top, assessing our situation. We were surrounded by flames, and flames were even beginning to descend through the ceiling vent, which meant the roof was also on fire. The only thing keeping us from turning to charcoal was the flame-resistant ceramic tile in the bathroom and the pathetic spray of water from the shower nozzle.

Flo said something I couldn't hear. "What?" I yelled back. She said it again. "What?"

She wrapped her free arm around me and buried her face into my neck. "I love you, kid," she hollered.

I felt the panic well in my throat. Flo is giving up. If Flo is giving up it must be bad. "What's that?" I asked.

"I said I love you," she repeated.

"I mean what is that sound? Do you hear that?" I continued to spray the flames with the shower hose, but it was like spitting on a campfire, at best it was barely delaying the inevitable. Then there was the sound again. Was it . . . was that a *car horn*?

Suddenly the Humvee crashed through the wall of the bedroom like a military tank, which, come to think of it, is kind of what a Humvee was. The ceiling collapsed on top of it in a cascade of burning beams and plywood, not making a dent, not even slowing it down as it pulled up flush next to us and the door sprang open.

"Get in!" we heard Ms. Washington scream from behind the wheel.

No need to tell us twice. Flo and I both flew through the open door and barely had time to shut it before the tank ground into reverse and we barreled backward out the opening, over the shrubbery, and into the neighbor's rosebushes. Ms. Washington shifted into drive and annihilated the rest of the landscaping as we tore out of there. When we passed the blaring fire trucks speeding in the other direction on the way to where we just came, the three of us were screaming at the tops of our lungs—from panic, fear, exhilaration, joy, you name it, we were screaming.

Flo and I both descended into fits of coughing. When we finally recovered, I climbed into the backseat and Flo remained up front. "What the hell are you doing driving this thing?" Flo wiped tears from her eyes and smiled at Ms. Washington. "Where's Scooter?"

"He was inside Starbucks taking forever," Ms. Washington said breathlessly. "He left your phone in the car, and you kept sending texts, and I didn't think you had time to wait for him to get back. The keys were in the ignition so I just took off! When I got there I saw the place was on fire. I couldn't believe how quickly it spread! I could see the two of you through the bedroom window, on the other side of the flames. There was no fire truck in sight so I just gunned it!"

She swerved to the right a bit and took down a road sign like it was a dried weed. "Oops," she giggled.

"Ms. Washington," I laughed, "be careful."

"My name is Anita."

We were still punch drunk as she popped a curb and traversed an irrigation ditch to pull into the Starbucks parking lot and screech to a stop next to a frowning Roundtree, who was holding a venti latte and tapping his foot impatiently. "Get in," Anita hollered at him. Surprisingly he climbed into the backseat without complaint. As he settled himself next to me he sniffed the air with consternation.

"Flo," he chided, "have you been smoking in my car again?"

"I guess you could say that," Flo said, and we three collapsed into laughter again, which was brought to another level when Trixi wrestled free from her protective wrapping to spring into Roundtree's lap, upsetting his treasured beverage.

But the giddiness was short-lived. Soon the gravity of our situation descended back upon us. After explaining what happened at the house, the question of going to the police was raised again. Anita exited at the next off ramp and pulled over.

"Let's assess our situation," she said. Did she really say that? (I couldn't believe she said that.) Roundtree's radio popped and crackled softly behind her. You'd think he'd have a decent antenna on this thing, I thought. This car probably only cost about a billion dollars. "The dog," Anita continued. "Why do you think they need the dog?"

"I've thought about that," I said. "Hackman said they didn't need the dog alive, so maybe he thinks she ate something. I mean, when we walked inside she was in the hall closet, which must have been new because obviously she'd been living on whatever scraps were laying around the house until then, and when those ran out she was resorting to anything chewable—pizza containers, potato-chip bags, mail . . ."

"Maybe she ate an important letter," Roundtree surmised.

"I doubt it," Flo responded, lifting Trixi, who wriggled like a darling, yipping little squid. "Look at her, she's half the size of a hamster. The only reason she didn't starve is probably because of how little food she needs."

"Well," Anita said as she shifted the car back into gear. "Guess we need to feed her some canned pumpkin."

"What? Why?" I asked.

"Child, seriously, have you not heard of the effects of canned pumpkin on the canine intestinal system? Three bites of this stuff and whatever's inside that fluffy little mutt will come shooting out like liquid lightning."

Roundtree groaned and dropped his head into his hands.

CHAPTER 7

Forty-five minutes later we were in the parking lot of the nearest Kroger. Flo and I sat on the Humvee's open tailgate sucking on popsicles to soothe our smoke-sore throats while Roundtree had found another Starbucks and was off ordering another ridiculous $8 concoction. "I can't watch this," he'd grumbled as he left.

Anita was in the backseat gently feeding Trixi another plastic spoonful of canned pumpkin. The poor pup was so starving she hardly needed coaxing. The can was twice as big as she was, but she was halfway through it and still eating when the stuff started coming out the other end. Luckily Flo had thought to buy pee pads and line the seat before Fifi Trixibelle's feasting began.

"Who wants to dig through the poo?" Anita asked, offering a plastic spoon in our direction. Flo and I looked at each other expectantly. "C'mon, you're the flight attendant," I told her. "You dig through crap all the time."

I was hardly exaggerating. It's stupefying all the stuff flight attendants are trained to deal with in the course of their professions. Flo alone has encountered enough heart attacks on her flights to fill an ER ward. People were constantly fainting, vomiting, explosive diarrhea-ing, and *dying* onboard planes inflight. Because where did they have to go up there? It's not like each airplane had an emergency room like they probably should, though recently the airlines had added defibrillators on each of the planes in their fleets and now flight attendants were required to complete annual training on how to use them. I was only bringing this up to demonstrate that Flo had a lot more experience with handling bodily fluids than I did.

"Fine," Flo grumbled, then snatched the spoon from Anita's hand and began her task. It didn't take long before she found something. "Uh, what's this?" Flo asked, lifting the spoon so Anita could get a better look. Roundtree, who was a few steps within reaching the car on his way back from his Starbucks mission, immediately turned around and began walking in the opposite direction.

"Looks like a piece of a postage stamp," said Anita. "Dogs like to eat the sticky stuff on the back sometimes." I smiled in agreement.

"You sure know a lot of trivial stuff," Flo told her.

"I like surfing the Internet at work so I can look busy while I'm ignoring all the customers in line at the DMV," Anita said.

"You'd make a good flight attendant," Flo complimented her. "Ignoring customers is my specialty. I don't even bother to look busy while I do it."

Both women laughed while Flo wiped the soiled stamp onto a napkin to set aside and continued her task. "Found something . . . it's a dime. Ooh, here's something . . . looks like the ear pad off a set of headphones. Okay, what's this? I think it's a button . . . yep, button . . ."

Roundtree had approached and retreated so many times during this interlude that it almost looked like he was walking in circles. His radio continued to crackle softly. I had no idea which station he was playing, but whatever it was I kept thinking I heard my name.

"Scooter, what's with your radio? Can't you get any tunes?" asked Flo.

"It's a police radio, Flo," he said impatiently.

"Wait, what?" I said. "Why didn't you tell us?"

"I use it for work," he said.

"You're an *entertainment* blogger," I said. "Why would you need a police radio?"

"I have my aspirations, you know," he said petulantly. "I don't want to always be writing about drunk-driving celebrities and poorly behaved heiresses and whatnot."

Poorly behaved heiress? I would have been rankled if I didn't suddenly feel bad for him. Who aspires to be a real journalist anymore? I thought. You may as well set your sights on becoming a chimney sweep or something. Sure, some probably still exist, but it's not like there's an overwhelming market for them these days, what with bloggers doing the job for free and no one giving a crap about the truth anymore. Flo often commiserated with me on the state of the news media.

"Ain't no such thing as journalism anymore," she would grumble, making sure to blow the smoke from her menthol away from my face. "These days it's just a bunch of baboons bloviating on the Internet. They should all go to the Middle East and get their heads whacked off like respectable reporters."

I peered at Roundtree from a distance and suddenly it occurred to me—the suit, the goatee, the comb-over, the gas-guzzling throwback for a vehicle; Roundtree was the epitome of old school. Even his name, "Roundtree," like a character in a Dickens novel. I wouldn't be surprised if he made it up as a pseudonym for future novels. It occurred to me he hadn't asked a single paparazzi-type question this whole evening. In fact it appeared as though he were doing his best to keep from interfering with events as they transpired, like he literally handed over the wheel to us and took a backseat to better be an objective recorder of events. Begrudgingly I realized it couldn't hurt to have someone like him on our side. Still, though, he did nickname me "Crash" and the moniker stuck. He was far from getting a free pass in my book.

I decided to keep my mouth shut and continued to crane my ear toward his radio. Flo and Anita discerned that all foreign objects had been effectively ejected from Trixi's anus, so Anita gathered everything and headed back to Kroger to use the bathroom to toss the excrement and wash off the contraband.

"There it is again," I said, pointing to the radio.

"What?" asked Flo.

"I swore I heard my name."

Roundtree hurried over and reached through the driver's side window to turn up the radio.

Attention all cars in Fulton County, the dispatcher buzzed, *again, be on the lookout for a female subject, approximately 16 years old, five feet ten inches tall, long brown hair, khaki cargo pants and brown hooded sweatshirt. She was last seen in the Milton Parkway area and is wanted for questioning in connection with a possible murder, home invasion, and arson. Two witnesses report she was seen entering the residence of one Morton Colgate at 801 Milton Chase Way in the Milton Chase subdivision of Alpharetta. The subject's name is April Mae Manning. Should you catch sight of subject, use extreme caution to apprehend immediately, she is considered armed and dangerous.*

Roundtree turned to me with a look of sheer excitement. "See?" he clapped his hands and pointed. "You *are* a fugitive!"

"Scooter, get in the car," Flo demanded. He hopped in the backseat just as I closed the hatch and lay flat on the back floorboard. Flo gunned it to the Kroger entrance just in time to catch Anita on her way back from the restroom. "Get in, girl! Hurry!"

Anita jumped into the front seat with a hoot of excitement. "What now?"

"The police have a BOLO out on April. They think she set the fire and killed Malcolm's dad."

"Why? What . . . how?"

"Evidently they have two asshole witnesses who said so."

We all knew who those witnesses were—Hackman and Ash. They must have made good on returning to the rubble to dig out what they wanted from the ashes, only to find that we'd escaped and taken Trixi with us. I closed my eyes and tried to rest while Flo uncharacteristically followed the traffic laws with agonizing precision. The Humvee was enough of an attention magnet on its own; add frantic driving and we'd probably be swarmed with SWAT helicopters within minutes. Flo threw her cellphone out the window as we entered the freeway in case Hackman alerted the police that she may be accompanying me. No need to be concerned about the phone belonging to Roundtree since Hackman had no reason to expect we'd be with him. I watched the stars in the night sky as we seemed to crawl down the highway at the pace of a herd of pachyderms. I didn't even have to ask Flo where we were going. I knew we were headed straight to Otis's place.

CHAPTER 8

Uncle Otis was standing in his driveway when we arrived. He had a police radio, too, and wisely knew not to call Flo in order to avoid having her cell ping off a nearby tower, thereby enabling the police to triangulate our position. Instead he simply expected us to come, and we did. Flo had barely braked to a stop before the doors flew open and we clamored out of the car.

"Flo!" Otis exclaimed pleasantly, his arms outstretched as he came toward her.

"Back off, Bluto," Flo held her arm outstretched and plowed past him. She called all of her ex-lovers "Bluto."

"Anita!" he extended her the same greeting, but got the same response, because Flo had told Anita everything about the philandering Otis during their bonding session over Trixibelle's pumpkin-poop episode in the back of the Humvee.

"April!" Otis turned toward me and I flung myself in his arms. "That's my girl!" he laughed. "Murder *and* arson. I'm so proud. Did you shoot Ash?"

Shooting people seemed to be Otis's answer to everything. Like me, Otis is into lists, and he has lists taped up all over the house: "Top 8 Reasons to Never Answer the Door," "5 Easy Ways to Disarm an Intruder," "4 Best Ways to Escape a Choke Hold," "9 Reasons Why You Should Shoot First and Ask Questions Later," and "The 8 Components to Optimum Situational Awareness."

If Otis ever actually shot anyone I never heard about it, though he did narrowly miss me once. He argued that I should not have been breaking into his home at the time. But what is a girl supposed to do when she lost her key and her uncle lives in an old biscuit factory with no doorbell? Besides that, he is the one who taught me how to pick locks in the first place.

Otis stepped into the role as my caretaker when my stepfather Ash was revealed to be the lying, thieving, heartless ball of buttholes I had been telling everyone he was since he lied and thieved his way into getting full custody of me a few years ago. But Fulton County family court moves like a comatose turtle. Waiting for it to correct a grievous mistake requires time-lapse photography and a hibernation pod. I mean, they *literally* found all the pieces of the bombed plane I was in, shipped them to Atlanta, and put them back together before a single status hearing was held on the subject of my custody. My only comfort is that Ash's spanking new wife Catherine, a WorldAir attorney as well as my former guardian ad litem to the court, did end up in prison for her part in the bombing and embezzlement attempt. She promptly annulled their marriage from behind bars and hasn't spoken to Ash since. This according to an article in the *Southern Times.*

Until today Otis was staying with me in my mother's townhome located in a swanky neighborhood just north of downtown Atlanta, which, if you ask me, was kind of like asking a spider monkey to watch over the animal lab. My mother is partial to pastels in her décor, and Otis blended in like a biker at a tea party. Steel-toed work boots, band-merch T-shirts, and grease-stained jeans was his staple ensemble. He used to wear his long curly hair in a ponytail until it got caught in the cooling fan of an engine he was working on. He was lucky there was a hacksaw within arm's reach so he could saw himself free before the engine ate his whole head. Today he wore his blond hair at chin level, just long enough to cover the two quarter-sized patches of bald spots from the incident. Oddly, it worked pretty well with the eye patch.

Otis turned to Roundtree and asked, "Who's this?" I introduced them and Roundtree, who held Trixi in one hand, extended the other to Otis, who shook it enthusiastically. "Nice white suit," he said.

"Nice black eye patch," Roundtree responded.

"Come on in. Can I get you a drink?"

"Do you have sherry?"

"Will tequila do?"

"Perfectly."

Flo had already opened the giant metal gate that was Otis's front door. As I mentioned earlier, Otis lived in a renovated old biscuit factory—a big concrete box, essentially, with 24-foot ceilings, giant clerestory windows, and leaking skylights. The entire structure was secluded by a forest of bamboo trees and accessible solely via an almost invisible easement alley. The front third of the building housed his machine shop, the middle third made up his living quarters, and the back third contained his exercise equipment, collection of sophisticated computers, security monitors, scanners, and 3D printers. The floor throughout was concrete, riddled with rusty tools and containing a drain in the center. This was his home. My mother referred to it as "Uncle Otis's House of Sharp Objects and Flame." When I was a toddler I wasn't allowed inside for fear I'd end up with a bunch of fishhooks in my head or something. As I got older it became one of my favorite places to hang out.

Otis closed and locked his gate and followed us through the covered alleyway that was his living room. He gathered us around his kitchen island, poured five shots of tequila, drank two, then dispensed the rest. "So," he said, "what the hell is going on?"

It was left to me to recount the night's events, seeing as how I was the only one not drinking tequila. Anita had one shot and was looking all wonky, flushed and smiling. Flo matched Otis shot for shot, and probably had half a flask of vodka from her purse as we spoke. It was well known she could rival Otis in the drinking department any day of the week. Roundtree belted his first shot and then sipped his second like it was a fancy liqueur. Fifi Trixibelle curled up in a soup mug on the counter and fell asleep, snoring surprisingly loudly for such a miniature dog. Mr. Colgate's suit jacket lay on the floor in case any more canned pumpkin rumbled forth from her bum.

Once I finished filling Otis in, he asked to see the objects we'd extricated from Trixi. I lay the four items on the counter and noticed that Anita had done an admirable job of scrubbing them clean. "Anything else?" he asked. "Anything from the house?"

I remembered the handgun, pulled it from my cargo pocket, and placed it on the counter. At the sight of the gun, Roundtree belted back the rest of his tequila.

"That's it?" Otis questioned me.

I remembered the notepad and baggage claim check, pulled them from my pocket, and also placed them on the counter.

"Where'd you get these?"

"They were on the kitchen counter next to the phone at Hackman's place," I answered.

"Actually," Anita held up her finger, then brought it to her lips to suppress a dainty burp. "Actually, the police dispatcher said the house belonged to Morton Colgate."

"Yeah," said Flo. "That's right. Why is that?"

"It can't be. Malcolm's dad lives—lived—in Los Angeles," I said. "I mean, that's the reason Malcolm was always having to fly cross-country, because his parents shared custody."

"Let's look it up," Otis said, opening his laptop. We told him the address and he entered it into some site that spat forth information on these things. "Yep, it says here that the house was bought by Colgate Enterprises, but then it was quitclaimed to someone else."

"What's 'quitclaimed'?"

"It refers to when the owner of a piece of property transfers all interest of the property to someone else. Basically it means he bought the house for someone else."

"Does it say who?"

Otis scrolled further down the screen. "Yes. Molly Hackman."

"Molly?" Flo and I exclaimed simultaneously. Why would Mr. Colgate buy Molly a big-ass house?

"I bet they were having an affair," Flo said.

"Um hmm, girl, you know it," Anita clicked her glass with Flo's and threw back another shot.

In some ways it made sense, and in others not at all. For one, it would explain why Hackman was so furious at Molly when she left him, and why his revenge against Mr. Colgate was meted out so viciously. But then what was this business about kidnapping Malcolm? And Trixi? What was with the dog? And what did Ash have to do with anything? And who was the blonde woman present during Malcolm's abduction? I voiced all these questions to the others at the round table, but they were so certain illicit sex was behind everything that they barely gave my thoughts any weight.

All but Roundtree. He put down his shot glass and eyed me intently. "She's right," he said. "An affair doesn't answer all the questions. We should look more closely at those photos I took during Crash's driving test."

"Let me get you your phone," Flo got up to retrieve her purse.

"Stop, I stole it back from you hours ago," he said, producing the phone from his pocket. Flo, nonplussed, sat back down and finished her tequila.

Otis uploaded Roundtree's photos and brought them up on his 30-inch computer monitor. We gathered around to peer closely at the details. He clicked through the day's earlier images until we got to the first one that showed us in Otis's old BMW outside Colgate Enterprises. "Oh, by the way," I said, "sorry about your car."

"No problem. A flame of glory—it could not have hoped for a better demise." He zoomed in on the silver Rolls-Royce in the photograph. "Do we know whose car this is?"

I was about to tell him it was Mr. Colgate's car, but come to think of it I wasn't sure whose it was. As far as I knew, Colgate lived in California, and I assumed he used company cars while in town to check on his Atlanta operations. Last year during my days as an unaccompanied minor flying from coast to coast to fulfill my own ridiculous court-fortified custody schedule, I'd used the onboard WiFi to look up the troubles

Mr. Colgate faced with the IRS. Poor Malcolm, I'd thought. The most detailed article appeared in *Forbes*, which informed that Colgate's troubles started when his ex-wife turned him in to the IRS and then to the FBI, as there were also some accusations that he had misled shareholders and engaged in other nefarious activity. At present not only had Colgate been indicted for tax fraud, but he was also under investigation for embezzlement, insider trading, and money laundering. If you asked me, it was a miracle that he'd escaped incarceration so far, though ironic to note that if he had been in a cushy federal prison right now he might still be alive today.

"What's the license number?" Anita asked.

"What?" We all turned to her.

"The tag number of the Rolls-Royce," she reiterated, "what's the number?" She huffed impatiently. "Never mind, move," she instructed Otis, who leaned to one side so she could access his keyboard. A few rapid strokes later we were looking at the DMV government employee interface. Within seconds she had pulled up the registered owner of the Rolls. Otis's eyes widened lasciviously. Stuff like this was catnip to him. I imagined the leverage he could garner against people by accessing this private information.

"There, see?" Anita pointed to the screen. "It was not a company car for Colgate Enterprises."

No, it was a company car for WorldAir.

"This doesn't mean anything," I ventured, a glint of company loyalty bursting to the surface. "They could have stolen the car."

"Who steals a silver *Rolls-Royce*?" Flo asked. She had a point.

"I totally would," Otis mumbled.

"Hackman is the liaison for the mechanics union, maybe that was part of the deal he brokered during contract negotiations." Now I was the one who had a point. It would not have surprised anyone that the self-serving Hackman had put his oily thumb on the scale to include perks like this for himself while the threat of a strike loomed heavily in the air and the other mechanics worried about making mortgages.

"Look at the knockers on that broad," Otis broke the silence. He pointed to the bombshell clutching Malcolm's arm in the picture.

"I know, right?" said Anita. "It's like she needs a bicycle pump for those puppies."

For all we knew she had a face like a frying pan, because none of the frames came close to catching her mug. Could it have been Malcolm's mother? I thought. I knew it was a long shot, because the last time I saw her she did not have blonde hair and weighed at least 20 pounds more than the person in the picture. But that was a while ago; she could have gone to Costa Rica and had the fat sucked out of her in that time. Who knew.

"Drag queen," said Roundtree. Our heads turned toward him in unison, like meerkats.

"Why do you say that?" Flo asked.

"Trust me," he assured. We didn't really.

Otis got up from the desk and returned to the kitchen island to assess the items retrieved from Trixi and the crime scene. He plucked a number-2 pencil from a cup on the counter and used it to shade the sheet. This outlined the impressions made from the note written on the previous sheet:

V-2927-PRES45

"What do you think that is?" I asked.

Otis shrugged. "It's a serial number for one of our airplane parts."

That made sense, since Hackman was an actual airplane mechanic. It was easy to forget he had a professional title other than Murdering Thieving Wife-Beating Kidnapping Odious

Arsonist Pig. I really didn't understand people like Hackman. He had a good job with a great company (when the CEO wasn't trying to sabotage it)—who could want anything more? My grandfather, who was secretly richer than any of us knew or could even imagine, loved to labor with his hands, as did all of my family members. Even Otis. Even me. The days I spent impersonating a flight attendant were way more fun than now, when I'm supposed to be waiting with bated breath on whether the court will deem me deserving of a huge fortune. The money wasn't a big deal—half the fun in life is figuring out how to get by without it. The only thing I cared about was if they were true, the rumors. I didn't know why it should matter—Roy Coleman was my grandfather regardless of whether we were connected by blood—but I just didn't want anything else taken from me for the time being. So I tried not to think about the impending court-ordered DNA test, the exhumation of my grandfather's grave, and the excruciatingly slow legal process of proving our genetic connection.

"Hey, April, where'd you go?" Otis asked, snapping his fingers before my face. I shook the cobwebs from my head and focused.

Otis held Trixi's button between his thumb and forefinger to peer at it closely. He picked up Colgate's suit jacket from the floor and examined it. It was a Brooks Brothers single-breasted jacket with peaked lapels and canvas lining. I know these things from the small selection of suits Officer Ned kept in his office. He liked to lecture me on their attributes as he removed the plastic from their trips to the dry cleaners. Colgate's jacket closed in front with one button, or it would have if the button wasn't missing.

Otis placed the button from Trixi against the buttonhole on the jacket. "Could be," he deducted. I thought it was curious that the button was not the two-hole or four-hole sew-through kind you'd normally find on expensive suits. Instead it was a teakwood toggle, with enamel ball caps on each end and a loop on the back used to attach it to the fabric. Otis plunked his toolbox onto the counter and began rifling through his heavy metal implements.

"Looking for a pickax?" Anita rolled her eyes. "Give it." She deftly snatched the button from him and opened a small eyeglass repair kit she'd rifled from her big purse. In it was the smallest screwdriver I'd ever seen. Otis left the room and came back with a giant industrial magnifying glass, the kind with a lighted halo and weighted base that comic book characters probably used during their experiments that turned them into supervillains. After Otis assured us it wasn't a death ray, Anita placed the button under the glass and we all gathered to look at its magnification.

"There," Otis pointed to a seam where the wood met the enamel ball cap. Anita gently pried the point of the jewel driver into the seam and the ball cap popped off. She handed the toggle to Otis, who upended it over the palm of his hand. Out came a tiny glinting rectangle, as thin as paper but stiffer, and about one and a half times the size of a grain of rice.

"What is that?" I asked.

"That," Otis frowned, "is a microprocessor."

"What's it for?"

"Let's find out." He carried it to a worktable covered in computer parts. I'd always assumed this material was like an ongoing art project or something, seeing as how several mobiles made from computer trace material hung throughout his warehouse. But it turned out a lot of this stuff had a use. Otis was like Captain Nemo that way. He rummaged through the stuff until he found an interface, popped something out, flicked it away, popped Trixi's microprocessor in its place, then inserted the interface as a whole into to the back of a hollow hard drive that had been sitting in the corner like a discarded old artifact. He hooked that up to another huge monitor then pushed the power button. Nothing happened. He pushed it again. Nothing.

"Is it plugged in?" I asked.

"Crap." He plugged it in and pushed the power button, and the monitor lit up like a police car.

"Why are the lights flashing?" I asked, then I realized it wasn't the monitor that was lighting up like a police car, but an actual police car that had pulled up in the easement alley behind Otis's warehouse. In a panic I dropped to the floor.

"Get under the table," Otis instructed me just as a helicopter searchlight flooded the room through the skylight above. Otis leaned back in his chair, shielded his eye, and waved to the pilot. A fleet of additional police cars, with lights and sirens blaring, clamored to a stop outside at the edge of the carport. Anita and Roundtree hastily sat down on the sofa and tried to look innocent. Flo seemed unaffected by the mayhem. She had returned to the end of the island where the other items from Colgate's place were laid out. She held the baggage claim ticket in one hand and Fifi Trixibelle in the other.

The sirens outside stopped, but the warning lights remained flashing as the shrill feedback of an activated megaphone pierced the silence. "This is the police," the officer began. No duh. "This is the police," he repeated. "We need everyone inside to vacate the premises immediately."

The floodlight from above shifted as the helicopter left to sweep the surrounding area. "Go!" prompted Otis, and I darted from beneath the table and down the basement stairs. The others followed me. Once downstairs, we huddled for a few seconds on what to do. It was Anita who suggested she and Roundtree turn themselves in, because "it's not like we did anything wrong." Outside we heard the officer tell his comrades to hold fire—*hold fire?*—and urged us once again to give ourselves up.

"Besides," she added, "I recognize the voice of the officer on the megaphone."

"Really? Who?" I asked.

"My boys are all police officers," she smiled.

"Ain't you full of surprises," Flo slapped Anita's palm soundly then hugged her goodbye. Anita took Roundtree's hand and they ascended the stairs together, their visages lit by the floodlight from the overhead helicopter.

"Wait! Take her." Flo rushed over and handed Trixi to Anita. The dog yipped excitedly and Anita put her in her purse as Otis closed and locked the door after them. It was an ironclad door fortified with a floor-mounted lock jamb. It might take a minute for the police to break it down, but no doubt they would.

"Wait," I cried. "Where's the microprocessor?"

"It's fine," Otis said.

"Where'd you put it?"

"Where do you think? I fed it back to Trixibelle."

Flo chuckled, "Good one," then she and I looked to Otis expectantly. Surely he would not have been a decent eccentric if he didn't have a secret passageway that led away from his property, right? Knowing Otis, there was probably an underground moat with a personal submarine waiting. Outside I could hear voices from the growing crowd of onlookers surrounding the scene. A news helicopter had already added to the noise coming from above, and I imagined that the news vans were probably jostling for as close a position as possible.

Otis retrieved a big box from his metal shelves and tossed it onto the floor. It contained a bunch of hard hats, jumpsuits with rubber waders, and reflective orange vests. He put a set on over his clothes and instructed us to do the same. Then he ran his hand along the brick foundation that made up the lower wall of the basement, came to a spot that seemed to satisfy him, and began pulverizing it with a sledgehammer.

"What are you doing?" I asked. "Where's the door?"

"There's no door," he said, taking another mighty swing. A brick broke free and fell to the dirt floor in a cloud of dust. Four more whacks and there was a hole the size of a sofa cushion. Otis activated the light on the brim of his hard hat and looked through the opening and smiled. To me, though, there was nothing but blackness on the other side.

"Go," he waved us inside. We hurried through even though we had no idea why, but the police were beginning to break down the front door above us so we didn't ask questions. Once we were all through the wall I was surprised to see that we could almost stand upright in the opening.

"What is this?" I asked.

"It's a coal reservoir," he answered. "In the past, all the factories on this street were connected by a common coal hole. It was easier for when the truck made a delivery, they only had to pour the coal down one chute."

"There are no other factories on this street," I reminded him. About a decade ago, his neighborhood had been targeted by gentrification and code enforcement, resulting in the outbreak of ice-cream-colored new buildings surrounding him now ("An infection of yuppie huts!" he liked to rail).

"Right, all the factories burned down. It's not really a good idea to connect a bunch of factories to a common fuel source, is it?"

Otis scuttled around in the reservoir, his feet crunching over the bits of coal that had probably been there for over a hundred years, until he reached the far wall. He ran his hand over it until he found another satisfying spot, and began thwacking that with the sledgehammer as well. Soon another hole was formed, and the three of us crawled through it to another cavern of blackness, and then another, and so on, until finally we reached one where Otis stopped pounding the bricks and instead started pounding a metal hatch about shoulder level above the ground.

"What's that?" I asked.

"It's the old coal chute," he said. The door gave way after the third whack, and we helped Flo through first, then me, then Otis crawled though on his own, and fairly swiftly for a guy his age, I might add. Once he closed the chute behind him, I turned around to find that we were in the well-organized basement of someone's home. Otis intuited my question. "Yeah, a lot of the yuppie huts on this street repurposed the foundations of the old structures."

"Someone's upstairs," Flo whispered.

"Let's leave then," he said, removing his hat. He stepped out of his coveralls and left them folded on a nearby utility shelf. Flo and I followed suit. Then Otis casually climbed the stairs into the house. Flo and I followed him with trepidation. Upstairs, three stoned teenaged boys were watching *American Horror Story* on television, either oblivious to or uncaring about the police and helicopter lights swarming the air outside their windows.

As we passed through the living room, one of the boys took a hit off his bong, inhaled deeply, and waved to us in greeting. "Otis," he nodded, exhaling the smoke.

"Trevor," Otis nodded back. "Is your mom home?"

"She's outside taking in the sights."

"Keys?"

"On a hook by the kitchen door."

We emerged from the house to find ourselves half a block from Otis's warehouse, where, by the sound of things, the police must have successfully broken down his barricades. Before we could make it to the dilapidated truck that was to serve as our escape vehicle, we were descended upon by a TV news reporter who'd seen us leave the house. His camerawoman shoved her newscam in my face, and I was certain I was busted until the newsman thrust his microphone at me and asked, "Is it frightening to know that your neighbor may be involved in terroristic activities, arson, and murder?"

Later, when the clip went viral and the newsman was ridiculed out of his job for not recognizing me as the suspect at the center of all the mayhem, my eyes were as wide as dinner plates when I mumbled, "No comment."

Flo and Otis each placed a hand on my shoulder, turned me away from the camera, and guided me through the crowd of bystanders to the truck, where we all piled into the front bench seat. "Where to?" he asked.

"The airport," Flo replied, producing from her purse a pack of cigarettes and then the ticket I'd found at Colgate's house.

"Oh, good, you got the baggage claim ticket," I said, recalling that Ash had said he needed it for something.

"It's not for baggage, it's for remains," Flo said as she lit her cigarette and inhaled.

"What?"

"It's not for a suitcase," Flo spoke louder this time, releasing the smoke from her lungs. "It's for a coffin."

CHAPTER 9

Before we reached the airport, we exited onto Virginia Avenue and pulled over so I could crawl into the small storage area behind the bench seat so Otis could sneak me inside the WorldAir employee parking lot. I had a badge of my own now—as opposed to the past, when I had to impersonate my flight attendant mother to gain access to the underbelly of the concourse—but I couldn't risk using it to enter the employee parking lot for fear the police would be alerted. Security guards stop each auto entering the parking lot to swipe our cards through a magnetic reader, much like a credit-card transaction, and just like a credit-card transaction it's a sure-fire way to triangulate someone's whereabouts.

"What about you?" I asked Otis. Obviously the police were in pursuit of him as well.

"Me? I never use my own." He opened his glove compartment to reveal a small collection of airline-employee badges.

"You have a bunch of counterfeit badges?" I marveled.

"These aren't counterfeit." He feigned offense. "These are authentic. They all work perfectly."

I should not have been surprised that Otis had a connection inside security that supplied him with newly minted badges. They were probably only good for a small window of time, and needed to be renewed periodically. I made a mental note to inform Officer Ned about this on a need-to-know basis. Otis handed a badge to Flo.

"This badge is for an African-American man," she objected.

"Close enough. They never look," Otis reminded her. "As long as it swipes clean they don't care."

"You're right." Flo clipped the badge to her collar.

"Why don't I get one?" I asked. "Why do I have to hide? Wait, never mind." I ducked back down. I'm the famous poorly behaved heiress, that's why. Thanks, Roundtree.

We sailed through parking-lot security and pulled into a space at the back of one of the bus stops. WorldAir utilized an employee bus system, collecting workers at designated spots throughout the massive parking property. Those buses then deposited the workers at different concourses throughout the Atlanta airport. For example, if a flight attendant needed to sign in for an international flight, she would catch the bus that took her to the belly of E or F Concourse. Flight attendants with domestic destinations go to a different location, and baggage handlers somewhere different still, and so on. I wasn't sure where Otis planned for us to go, especially since I had no badge, but then Flo grabbed one from his glove compartment and clipped it to my shirt with the picture facing inward.

"No one ever asks," she said, referring to an airline security protocol in which employees are required to stop anyone without clearly visible ID to produce their badge on demand.

She was wrong, though. I knew three people at least who would demand ID without hesitation: Officer Ned, LaVonda, and me. We couldn't be the only ones, but Flo is right in her inference that security measures have become generally complacent at WorldAir.

Each parking stop offered a covered shed that housed a community bulletin board, where employees pinned announcements that covered everything from cars for sale, missing pets, places for rent, uniform pieces for trade, etc. I noticed two missing-person posters, which were by themselves not unusual. Airline employees were a natural resource for finding missing persons, because often it turns out the people were missing on purpose and trying to get out of town, but what made these posters unusual was that the missing persons *were* airline employees. "Have You Seen John Lassateur?" one read above the face of a smiling white male in his thirties. A large wine-colored birthmark covered the left side of his neck and jaw. "He was last seen entering the employee parking lot on Thursday, March 27. If you have any information or know of his whereabouts, please contact . . ." A bus pulled to a stop in front of us and the driver opened the door.

"Hi, Otis," she said.

Otis sprang onto the platform ahead of us and engaged the diminutive, sweet-natured driver in an animated conversation about how cancer was really the result of a government chemical experiment gone awry. She happily bantered with him on the subject while Flo and I slinked into the empty bus behind Otis and sat down. Soon Otis took the seat in front of us and we were on our way.

When the bus cleared the last security hurdle and rolled onto the tarmac to join the buzzing hive that made up the bedrock of the Atlanta airport, I sat back and relaxed for the first time since that morning. For all its flaws, WorldAir was a haven for me. In the past it provided a port in the storm when my world was upside down—dead father, institutionalized mother, sociopathic criminal for a stepfather. For me, the WorldAir employee lounges provided a place of stability and escape. The employees themselves were like a league of comrades. I loved being part of it, even if my connection at the time was deceitful. The crisp uniforms, the employees with purpose, the order, the accountability—even if it was a false front, it created an atmosphere in which I could breathe easier and calm down.

"You okay?" Flo asked. I straightened immediately. *Christ,* I thought, *I'm crying.*

"Just thinking about Malcolm," I told her and collected myself.

She put her arm around me and took a drink from her flask of vodka. "Everything's gonna be . . . wait, why are we stopping?"

Otis stood up to assess the situation, just as the driver opened the bus door. "Hi, Hackman," she said pleasantly. "What happened to your arm?" Hackman answered by reaching in his lunch box, retrieving a firearm, and shooting her in the face.

Flo and I screamed, sprang from our seats and ran to the rear of the bus. Otis roared in anger and dove toward Hackman, hitting him in the midsection. A wild shot rang out and ricocheted around the bus interior, grazing my hair. I flipped the latch on the emergency window exit and almost broke my foot trying to kick it open. Flo was already trying on the other side, with equal futility. Just our luck—rusted shut.

Hackman tackled Otis and they both flew onto the massive dashboard of the bus, pummeling each other with blows. The poor bus driver wilted lifeless in her seat while the two men did their best to kill each other. As they tumbled onto the aisle, Otis hit and kicked at Hackman's gun hand viciously. Hackman held on, though. It was dark outside as well as inside the bus. The whole while motorized luggage tugs were zipping around us like oblivious birds. If anyone was suspicious of an employee bus sitting at a cold stop along the tarmac, it wasn't evident. Other buses seemed to circumvent us without a thought, and no aircraft was in imminent need of us to move in order to clear a gate. Two more bullets fired, creating a deadly dodgeball effect for me and Flo. I pulled the lever on the emergency roof exit and thankfully it gave way.

The rooftop emergency exit on a bus like this was about the size of a toilet seat. Ever since they abolished the weight limit for flight attendants in the early nineties, some of them took that as freedom to explore their inner plus-sized model—and good for them—but I always wondered what would happen to them in a situation like this one, when our only option was to shimmy through a hole in the roof hardly big enough to allow a giraffe to poke through his head. I'm skinny but gangly, and I bruised my hip bones badly while pulling my way through. Tiny Flo, on the other hand, sailed up and out like a Romanian acrobat, of course. I swear all that tobacco and alcohol were toughening her up like dried horsehide. Once on the roof, we stood up only to have the bus literally squeal away from underneath our feet. The two of us stumbled, then fell, then rolled off the back of the bus. I hit the ground first, like a sack of wet cement, and broke Flo's fall.

We lay groaning on the ground as the bus barreled into the distance without us. We had no idea who was behind the wheel or even if Otis was still alive. After what seemed like forever, an ambulance finally came skidding to a halt in front of us. Thank God, I thought, waving to the driver to help. The driver leaned on his horn and hollered out his window. "What the hell are you doing in the middle of the taxiway? Get out! We have an emergency to get to!"

The instant we inched out of the way, the ambulance whizzed past us. I sat back down on the tarmac to catch my breath, while Flo pulled on my arm in a futile attempt to get me to move. More work vehicles barreled by, followed by honks and curses of the drivers. A few moments later I regained my strength, and started to run in the direction in which we'd last seen Otis, but Flo called to me to stop.

"Kid, look." She pointed to a tug train pulling four flat carts. The last of the carts contained, in three stacks of two, six identical air trays, or CCUs as they're known in the industry, which stands for "casket combination units." It's the only way WorldAir will ship human remains. I set out for them in a dead run.

CHAPTER 10

Here's why I was terrified at the thought of my friend Malcolm in combination with a baggage claim for a casket—I mean besides the obvious. First, human remains are not allowed to be transported by air unless the container is hermetically sealed. Which means that anyone with ideas to stow away on a cheap flight to Fiji by booking themselves as human remains better know how to hold their breath for hours at a time, otherwise they're going to arrive looking like a mummy that got sealed in its sarcophagus a few years too soon.

The same goes for anyone hoping to transport kidnap victims, if you ask me. I'm not an expert on this by far, but I do know that the airlines have spent untold hours thinking of ways a person can smuggle a breathing human across country lines, and still they haven't touched the tip of the Mt. Everest of ingenuity that is the human imagination. Last year a Cuban girl shipped herself to Miami inside a wooden crate via DHL, for chrissakes. The crate was no bigger than a two-drawer filing cabinet. She could not have possibly known whether the aircraft assigned to her freight load had a pressurized cargo area—some do and some don't. She was literally leaving her life to the wind.

Not everybody wins the crapshoot in that regard. I regularly rifled through the security alerts on Officer Ned's desk to read report after report depicting stowaway attempts by young people from impoverished countries who climb into the wheel wells of jetliners, hold on for takeoff, and expect to arrive alive at the other side of the hemisphere. First, it's a million degrees below freezing at 35,000 feet, with oxygen so thin you'll die from hypoxia before the first icicles form on your big dead face.

In the distance, I could see the tug train come to a stop along side a 737 connected to a gate near the end of B Concourse. A portable conveyor ramp had been set up underneath the plane, leading up to its open cargo door. The driver got out and began tossing suitcases and other items from the first cart onto the rotating belt of the conveyor ramp, which carried them to the top, where another ramp worker crouched inside the cargo bin caught them as they rolled off the ramp, then tossed them willy-nilly throughout the interior of the hatch. A lot of people think there are shelves or some other means of order in the cargo hatches of WorldAir passenger aircraft, but no. Like with most airline fleets, our aircraft cargo hatches are unadorned metal caverns where bags, boxes, packages, even pet carriers with pets inside, are flung one on top of another with all the care and symmetry you'd expect from a dump truck backing up to a landfill.

I reached the tug train before Flo. My fall from the bus had me moving stiffly but I did my best to shake it off. The tug driver wore regulation earplugs to protect his ears from the constant and deafening roar of the surrounding jet engines, so he was pretty much oblivious to any activity in proximity to his surroundings. See? Situational awareness. People wonder how mechanics and ramp workers get run over by slow-moving jets, but it happens all the time. Just recently a Boeing employee was run down by a brand-new jet backing out of the construction hangar. The jet was being pushed by a tow tug and only traveling five miles per hour, but those wheels are like giant balls of rubber quicksand; once one of them clips your foot or your coat tail it will suck the rest of you under with it. The driver of the tug was wearing earplugs, so he couldn't hear his coworker screaming at him to cut the engine.

I hadn't memorized the number on the claim ticket from Colgate's house, but at least I knew the casket we were looking for was traveling to Grand Cayman, an island in the British Antilles. The caskets were not all facing the same direction, and there was no uniform method for the ticketing agents in the cargo department when it came to sticking claim checks on crates, so my progress was hindered while I flailed around looking for identifying numbers. Flo reached my side just as the ramp agent had gripped one of the transport caskets from the baggage cart and maneuvered it onto the conveyor ramp.

"Wait!" we yelled to no avail. Earplugs, remember. I jumped onto the conveyor ramp and climbed onto the casket. The worker up in the cargo area caught sight of me and stopped the belt, leaving me perched halfway between the ground and the aircraft. He must have thought I was a grieving passenger, because it sounded like he was hollering condolences or something. I caught snippets of "onto a better place" and the like. The ramp agent at the bottom of the belt was not nearly as forgiving. "Get the hell off there!" the driver yelled, waving a crowbar at me. I ignored him and continued to search for the claim sticker. Flo snatched the crowbar from his hand and smacked him up against the head. A shouting match ensued. He must have known Flo personally because he threw up his arms, stormed back to his tow tug, and plunked down in the driver's seat with a huff. The ramp worker in the cargo belly, led by curiosity, stepped out onto the belt to begin his descent, but then tripped and stumbled madly toward me. He fell and barreled into the casket with a thud, knocking it off the belt and toward the tarmac below. It hit the concrete corner first and burst apart like it was built from balsa wood. A plastic-wrapped cadaver tumbled free from the planks. The clumsy ramp worker and I both ogled the scene in shock. He reached for me to steady himself, but instead knocked me off my feet and sent me over the edge as well. Luckily the corpse cushioned my fall.

The cadaver did not appear to be what Flo and I were looking for—not that we knew what we were looking for, but surely it wasn't this. The departed was a heavyset middle-aged woman who must have died in a car accident or something. She appeared to be wearing the clothes in which she perished, a pale blue pant suit mottled with blood and gravel. I would tell you what her face looked like if she had any of it left.

That was the thing with the transport of the deceased via air travel; most of the time the bodies were people who had died while away from home, and were dispatched straight from that county morgue to the mortuary in their hometown, where family members were awaiting a funeral. So, if there was a body being shipped in the belly of a plane, chances were it had yet to be touched by a mortician to make it look presentable. They were packed up and shipped fresh from the coroner's slab.

"Ugh," I grunted as I rolled off the body. The ramp worker above me was evidently so overcome that he fled back into the cargo area of the 737 and cowered there. I couldn't blame him.

"Great!" exclaimed his coworker, jumping down from the driver's seat in the tug. "Who's gonna clean this up?"

By now we'd caught the attention of passengers on the concourse above us. A crowd had gathered along the large window overlooking the tarmac, and people were snapping pictures with their cellphones. The ramp agent extended his hand to help me up and I rose shakily to my feet, only to be knocked down again by Flo, who had commandeered the luggage tug and drove it into me. Not hard, but still.

"Get in, Crash," she commanded. She did not have to tell me twice. She hit the gas and we drove off to the frustrated profanities of the ramp agent behind us. I looked back to register the four flat luggage carts still attached to the tow tug. The last two contained the five remaining transport caskets.

"Where to?" she asked.

"North 90," I answered.

CHAPTER 11

North 90 was short for "North 90 Virginia Loop," the address of a surplus hangar left over from the Second World War that was still located on the airport grounds, which by no means meant it was nearby. The Atlanta airport was the busiest airport in the world, and its grounds covered almost 133 square miles and spanned three separate city limits. (One tends to forget how huge these international airports actually are.) I knew North 90 was presently practically abandoned now that the repairs were finished with the aircraft it housed. I thought it would make a good place to pull in a tug train and pry open some coffins.

North 90 had undergone a number of renovations and uses over the decades, having been appropriated by a bevy of eye-blink airlines that have come into and gone out of business in that time. (Hooters Air, anyone?) WorldAir had owned it since the early fifties, and made good money leasing it to these corporations. During my brief tenure as a board member, I liked to dive into the company archives to look up as much of the history as I could. Much of this information was public information, but not attainable in digital format, which meant you couldn't find it online. These days if you can't click on something it might as well not exist. I know I sound like a get-off-my-lawn old fart when I say that, but it really does seem like the truth is not so much hard to find as it is just neglected and ignored. It was like catnip for me to forage through these records that hadn't been touched in half a century. Taped to the window frame above my desk in Officer Ned's office was a list of the six crazy fly-by-night airlines that WorldAir has leased North 90 to since the seventies.

6 CRAZY FLY-BY-NIGHT AIRLINES TO WHICH WORLDAIR HAS LEASED HANGAR SPACE

1. **Hooters Air**—The worst part of this airline, if you ask me, is that they made the public think the half-naked waitresses on board were actually flight attendants. They weren't. I'm surprised this airline lasted three years.
2. **Naked-Air**—This nudist airline existed exactly one day.
3. **Pet Airways**—For the kind of pet fanatics who serve their show dogs filet mignon.
4. **Erotic Airways**—The sole purpose of this airline was to indoctrinate willing partners into the Mile-High Club. The pilots didn't even log a destination when they took off. They just took off, circled around, and came back. It folded after four days.

5. **Smokers Express**—A smokers-only airline that didn't even last a day. The executive who thought of it couldn't get the backing to get it off the ground.
6. **Argyle Air**—This was started by a company known for its clothing, which I guess is just as good as an airline started by a company known for its hot wings.

Today North 90 was being used to repair the infamous L-1011 that fell apart above Albuquerque last year. You'd think that crashed-up airplanes would go straight to the scrapyard, but banged-up aircraft are salvaged all the time. In the eighties a Boeing 737 crashed in the Andes mountains, killing half the people aboard and completely shearing off the left wing and landing gear. That aircraft was cargoed off to the salvage yard and welded to the remains of others to make an airworthy facsimile of itself. Typically it was then sold to a lesser airline, as it was unusual for a major airline to reintegrate a crash-repaired airplane back into its own fleet. Maybe the reason for this had something to do with superstition—that or the fact that, holy crap, the plane frickin' fell apart and crashed in a former life.

This L-1011 in particular was slated to be sold to a puddle-jump startup based in Grand Cayman called Peacock Airways. As a condition of the sale of the L-1011 to Peacock Airways, WorldAir was only responsible for restoring the structure to airworthiness, which is why zero restoration had been made to the interior of the fuselage. Airlines, when they buy a brand-new plane, get them delivered gutted so they can retrofit the interior with their patented seats, systems, and décor. Since Peacock Airways was buying this plane used, they would have to do the gutting themselves.

The L-1011 airplane was a good candidate for reconstruction, seeing as how the bomb blast had been isolated to the tail section, which broke off cleanly for the most part. Otis himself had been instrumental in reattaching a replacement tail section, as he could not resist anything that required the use of fire and hanging from a harness. (My heart felt a pang of worry as I wondered what came of him. I hoped he was able to crush Hackman's face like a bug.)

Peacock Airways itself had only been in existence for less than a year and was already off to a bad start. For its ceremonial inaugural flight, packed with politicians and media, the Caribbean PR department for the airline thought it would be a good idea to let loose a flock of actual peacocks to roam the aisles of the plane and entertain the passengers. I guess nobody told them that peacocks are pretty vicious birds. One bit a fingertip off of a local television reporter, which caused the passengers to panic and run to the front of the aircraft to get away from the birds. The sudden redistribution of weight caused the pilot to lose control of the airplane, which immediately crashed just off the shore of Cancún. You can see a number of videos of the crash on YouTube, even, thanks to the gaggle of tourists on the beach with their cellphones at the ready. Four passengers and most of the peacocks died.

That Peacock Airways was still in business is testimony to the complacency of the traveling public, if you ask me. Most people didn't seem to care about the condition of the plane, or even of the pilot, they just wanted to pay as little as possible for a ticket to Vegas. I attributed this mentality to a theory I had about the perpetuation of mass delusion put upon consumers by the airline industry as a whole. Because in fact it was not normal to be rocketing around in a metal tube thousands of feet above the ground. We all know it's not normal, but just as people are able to be incited to panic about innocuous things, they can be placated from panicking about things that are anything but innocuous. I once wrote a paper for my online high-school psychology class that centered on that famous case in the sixties in which a woman was stabbed to death over the course of 45 minutes on the street outside her apartment building. Several of her neighbors heard her screams, but did nothing because, surely, if something frightening was happening, wouldn't everyone be jumping from their seats to make a fuss? Normalcy is an artificial and self-fulfilling construct. The neighbors weren't evil people, they were just adjusting to the present circumstances with bovine complacency.

Airlines depended on bovine complacency in order to exist. They fortified it with all the inflight distractions available in recent decades—sound-canceling headphones, eye masks, nonstop movies, inflight WiFi, *alcohol*—all these conveniences perpetuated the illusion that it was normal to be hurtling through the sky in a metal vessel that was one burnt-out wire away from being a smoldering black crater in a cornfield somewhere. In truth it made perfect sense to be terrified to fly, but the artificial normalcy maintained that there was nothing to be frightened about. Because, surely, if something frightening was happening, wouldn't everyone be jumping from their seats to make a fuss?

See? Situational awareness. The airlines had discovered it could work for and against them.

When Flo and I pulled into the hangar, the lights were dimmed as the mechanics had gone home, though a pair of lunch boxes remained on the picnic table outside the utility office on the right side of the building. Behind the Plexiglas, a security guard leaned way back in an office chair with his back to us and his feet up on the desk. The hangar was so large it could house an entire neighborhood. So large, in fact, that WorldAir opted to place only a single security camera at the entrance of the facility, then sprang for the round-the-clock security officer to address any unlikely intrusions.

Flo directed the tug train toward the starboard side of the mammoth aircraft, the side farthest from the security guard, who hadn't looked up from his nap. She parked it so that the last trailer was blocked from view by the giant wheel of the back landing gear. She braked the vehicle and I hopped off in a rush toward the caskets. Flo was right behind.

"Where the hell are the ID stickers?" I griped.

"Who cares," Flo said, thwacking the first crate with the crowbar she'd taken from the ramp worker. Splinters flew but the lid didn't budge.

"Give it," I took the crowbar and shoved the flat end into the seam of the lid and partially pried it open, then repeated the maneuver further down the crack until we could get enough leverage to pop open the lid. I didn't have to take a second look to know it wasn't what we were looking for. Inside the naked body of a heavily tattooed Hispanic man stared back at us, the Y-shaped coroner's incision traversing his lumpy, bloated torso. It looked like the coroner used kite twine to unevenly stitch it back together. This rankled a peculiar offense to my sense of decorum. "Oh my God, I hope after my autopsy they sew me up better than that."

"Promise me you'll bury me at sea," Flo said.

We shoved the crate off the trailer to make way for the one underneath. I cringed when it hit the ground with a crash, rolled on its side, and emptied its contents onto the floor. *Sorry,* I winced, grateful the body was encased in plastic. "Did we break him open? It looks like we broke him open."

"Focus, Crash," Flo reminded me. She'd adopted my technique with the crowbar and was halfway finished prying off the lid of the next casket. I placed my palms under the lip of the cover and shoved upward, popping it free. I looked away; inside was a girl who could not have been more than 19. Poor thing. She wore only blue panties. Her cause of death wasn't discernable from the outside.

The next casket held a guy who must have been in his seventies. The skin on his face and neck was speckled with dried blood, but other than that he looked like he was sleeping.

"Here goes nothing," Flo deftly pried open the next lid without my help. She was getting pretty good at it now. As soon as she flipped it open, the stench hit us in the face like a cloud of chemical toilets.

First, it's common for things to go awry during the international shipping of human remains, and this was a case in point. A hermetic seal is just a "tight seal," not necessarily an "airtight seal." And if left unattended in a warm climate, a hermetically sealed cadaver can slow-cook like one of those meals-in-a-sack you find in old army rations. I covered my nose and mouth with the crook of my arm and finally noticed the claim sticker on the bottom corner of the crate. It showed the cadaver had come in on a flight from GCM that night. It was hot in the Caribbean this time of year; this casket must have sat on the tarmac at Owen Roberts airport and stewed for a few hours before they finally loaded it.

"Looks like the same sewing technique as the first guy." Flo lit a cigarette and pointed to the coroner's incision. The corpse was a pot-bellied Caucasian male. He looked to be in his mid-thirties at the time of his death, which appeared to have been from two bullets to the head. His chin and neck were smeared with a big dark blood stain. He was clad in grotty boxer shorts and nothing else.

I looked more closely at the coroner's incision and yes, it was crudely stitched up like the last one. But then why wouldn't it be? County coroners are doctors who only deal with dead people, and most of the time their cases come to them as a result of some terrible crime. If they had to humanize their subjects they probably wouldn't be able to make it through the day. It's up to the mortician to dress the body up for burial, and it's not like they bother with anything under the clothes. I heard they use everything from PVC piping to chicken wire to chopsticks to position bodies so they look presentable for the funeral.

Flo rested against the crate and took another drag on her cigarette. I have to admit I was grateful for the smoke because it was helping to mask the ghastly reek coming from the casket.

"I think I know that guy," Flo joked wanly, pointing to the dead man, "if it wasn't for the beer gut."

In fact his gut was so huge it looked like he swallowed a medicine ball. My eyes must have been playing tricks on me, because his belly seemed to get bigger by the second. Later, thinking back on this moment, I had to marvel again about how, just when I think I'm jaded enough not to be surprised at any terrible turn of events, just when I think I've hit rock bottom, a trap door opens to reveal a whole other level of awfulness beyond anything I can imagine.

Flo sensed it before I did, and tentatively placed her hand on my elbow as she backed away from the casket. I should have trusted her instincts, but instead I peered closer at the bloated corpse. My brows furrowed. It appeared as though the tension against the stitches was causing them to come undone. "What the . . . is that . . ."

Boom! The cadaver exploded like a loaded cigar. Thick, rust-colored gore coated the interior of the not-so-carefully sealed hermetic bag. Luckily the thick plastic kept most of it from splattering all over us like gut stucco, but believe me, enough got out to send Flo and me scuttling to the other side of the wheel well to escape the scene.

"What the hell was that?" Flo lit another cigarette, her hands shaking.

"Jesus God," I gasped.

I think I knew what happened. My mother was a fanatic about those forensic shows that detail terrible rapes/homicides/abductions and crimes of the like, and often forced me to watch them with her so she could point to the screen and exclaim, "See? Never go near a man in a van!" or "What'd I tell you? Never answer the door!" I remember one show steered from the norm by investigating a funeral home in Georgia where the director was caught ripping off the families of the deceased by not performing the services for which he'd been paid, I mean *at all*. People would drop off their loved ones for cremation, for example, and two days later the mortician would hand them a box of ashes that later proved to be nothing but incinerated kitchen garbage. Later the uncremated bodies were found dumped and rotting around the backyard, covered in tarps, leaves, and pieces of plywood.

For the deceased who were to forgo cremation and be buried after an expensive closed-casket ceremony, the shady mortician reserved a special kind of neglect. He just placed their remains in the casket and sprinkled a few pounds of ground coffee on top to try and dissipate the smell. Ground coffee used to be pretty effective at masking the scent of narcotics when smugglers tried to get past the drug dogs at customs, but it was less effective at camouflaging the reek of rotting flesh, and soon the funeral home was the subject of local suspicion. The suspicion instigated an official federal investigation during a somber funeral one hot day when the casket at the center of the ceremony very unceremoniously blew up like a bad parlor joke. It turned out that the body, a misanthropic spinster aunt whose estate everyone in the room was hoping to inherit, had not been embalmed at all, so it continued to decompose in the heat and accumulate trapped gases until the inevitable happened.

I started to explain this to Flo, but she remembered she'd seen the same episode and cut me off. "What are those, bones?" she pointed to a bunch of octagonal-shaped objects amid the sludge. They were not bones. They looked like plastic machine parts. There were a lot of them.

I poked at a few with the toe of one of my Doc Martens boots. *What the hell is that?*

"Are any more dead bodies going to explode?" Flo asked nervously. "Because if so, we need to maybe leave. I can handle a house fire, tunneling underground, homicide, what have you, but I don't think I can deal with any more juice from a dead guy getting on me just now. I have my limits."

"Me, too." There was still one casket that remained unopened, but the claim sticker I'd finally found on it showed that it had come into ATL that afternoon from JAX. The ticket we found at Colgate's house specified cargo that originated in ATL and was due to ship out to GCM tomorrow night. I took Flo's hand and we walked toward the security cubicle to wake up the guard, who was still napping like a big hibernating bear. I swear, sometimes I think WorldAir employees only come to work to get some rest. Flo would totally back me up on this. She herself loved to fly on aircraft like the very L-1011 in the hangar with us right now, where she could smoke, drink, and sleep off a bender in the privacy of the passenger-free lower galley.

On the picnic table outside the security window, one of the lunch boxes sat open exposing a number of used sandwich bags. So I grabbed a couple and quickly doubled back to the sack of muck that was now the poor pot-bellied guy. The WorldAir flight attendant training manual teaches you to collect contaminated items by putting your hand into a plastic bag as though it was a fingerless glove, plucking up the item, then turning the bag inside out so the item sat inside without your fingers ever having touched it. I collected a couple of those weird gadgets that were mixed in with the guts, then sealed the sandwich bag and put it into one of the pockets below the knee zipper of my cargo pants.

Heading back, I saw that Flo had yet to awaken the security guard. Instead she was leaned over his computer terminal, typing something on his keyboard. "What are you doing?" I whispered from force of habit. Someone was sleeping, after all. Then I remembered the whole point, and extended my hand toward his shoulder to shake him awake.

"Don't bother," Flo said. "He's dead."

"What? Why?" I implored. Flo shrugged and shook her head sadly, then she directed her attention back to the computer screen. Someone had shot the guard in the forehead and then placed his cap back on his head, propped his feet on the desk, turned off the light, and voilà, instant undiscovered homicide for a few hours at least, because since when was the sight of a sleeping security guard suspicious at all? Christ, I thought, the body count for today was really getting to be uncomfortable.

I crept to Flo's side and saw that she had entered the WorldAir employee interface and pulled up the information on the list of travel caskets scheduled to pass through the airport today and tomorrow. Since the caskets were considered cargo and not human beings, there was zero information on the identities of the deceased, only the identities of the people authorized to claim them. That day alone there had been eight travel caskets shipped to Atlanta on WorldAir; seven of them came from Grand Cayman, and one from Jacksonville. All of them had been authorized for pickup by the same person: Ash Manning.

CHAPTER 12

I slammed the desk in anger. I've known Ash since I was four years old, when he'd begun his campaign to ingratiate himself into the life of my newly widowed mother, who suffered under the impression I'd need a male authority figure in my home. Back then Ash was a blue-eyed, handsome, blond, fit pilot for WorldAir who made about a quarter million a year. My working-class mother was thrilled when he suggested he officially adopt me—that was, until he divorced her later. By documenting himself as my father via the legal adoption, and booting my mother out of the picture, he had positioned himself to be not only the executor of my estate but my next of kin, in line to get everything in the event of my demise. By the time I figured out what was happening I was in this airplane right here, literally minutes away from crashing. Luckily his plan was foiled and everything turned out happily ever after . . . *not.*

For some reason Ash was still at large, evidently with the blessing of the police, who'd refused to apprehend him after he'd broken into my house last year. My lawyer friend Alby looked into it and saw that this was due, in part, to the fact that the Fulton County court had yet to sign off on the petition she'd submitted on my behalf to remove Ash as my legal parental guardian. Therefore, when the police arrived after I'd called them, they stood down because the situation was considered a "civil matter" and not a criminal one. Still, this didn't explain why Ash was free to frolic all over Georgia committing arson and attempted murder and giving false statements to the police. Just last year he had been involved in the bombing of a passenger jet. That was a federal offense, right? Shouldn't they be waterboarding his worthless ass in Gitmo right now?

"I should have gone to Sweden," I'd heard Flo grouse many times about her connection to Ash. At first I thought she made this lament because Sweden had been historically more progressive when it came to the plight of single mothers. But recently Flo corrected me. "All I know," she said, exhaling a cloud of menthol smoke, "is that abortion was legalized there in 1938."

Ash had been fired from his pilot duties at WorldAir—at least there was that small consolation for the time being—but not banned from using the airline to travel as a passenger. Flo pulled up his travel information to show he was booked on a flight to Grand Cayman the following night.

Then she retrieved the pairing summary that detailed the flight crew, cabin crew, and aircraft type and number. I'm pretty versed with this interface, having been tutored by Flo, my mother, and a number of other flight attendants who relied on me to submit their scheduling requests throughout the month.

Looking at the pairing summary in regard to Ash's flight, I knew something was different right away. First, the flight number was way off sequence. WorldAir flight numbers all start with either a zero or a one, and none of them are over four digits long. This flight number began with a nine.

"Ah, charter flight," I remembered.

"Not only that, but it's a ferry," Flo added. A ferry flight is when the aircraft is being flown with just deadheading crew members and no paying passengers. Aircraft are transported this way for many reasons—perhaps they are broken but airworthy, or needed to be transported in order to pick up passengers who are stranded because their connecting flight is grounded with a mechanical problem, etc.

"If it's a ferry flight, then why is Ash booked on it? He's not a crew member anymore."

"He is, though."

"*What?*" I thought we fired his crooked ass. "I swear, if WorldAir has hired him back, I'll . . ."

Flo stopped me. "Crash, he's not part of the WorldAir crew. He's a part of the Peacock Airways crew." I looked closer. It was true. According to the seniority date depicted next to his employee number, Ash had been hired by Peacock Airways the previous September. Seriously? I thought. Do these people not perform background checks?

Flo pointed to the vessel number on the pairing summary, which indicated the airplane to be used on the flight. "Can you believe it?" The vessel number was that of the very L-1011 in the hangar with us now. Evidently Peacock planned to take possession of it tomorrow, and was having it delivered. Ash was piloting the plane to Grand Cayman.

Also booked on the passenger manifest, interestingly, were Mr. and Mrs. Morton McGill Colgate. I was more surprised that the two agreed to be in the same plane together than I was that they were registered on the flight in the first place. Colgate Enterprises owned a hefty amount of stock in Peacock Airways.

"Guess Mr. Colgate won't be making that flight," Flo intoned gravely. She pressed the "print" button at the top of the screen, and the old-fashioned dot-matrix printer sprang to life with a bunch of bleating screeches as it spat out the screen capture. I snatched the printout before it hit the tray, folded it, and put it in another of my pockets. I reminded myself to make sure to buy five more pairs of cargo pants if I ever survived this adventure. My new uniform, I thought. You could bury me in it.

Above the printer was another employee community bulletin board like those at each bus stop in the employee parking lot. I suddenly stood straight, snatched a paper off the wall, and turned to Flo. "What is it?" she asked.

I didn't respond. Instead I walked past her and ran back to the tug train we'd left on the starboard side of the L-1011. Flo followed me loyally but reluctantly, suggesting that maybe we should turn ourselves in now and let the authorities try to find Malcolm. It was saying something that Flo now wanted to entrust "authorities" with our task, since Flo had been instructing me all my life not to trust authority. One of the first things I remembered her telling me as a kid was, "If someone ever shows you a badge and tells you to leave somewhere with him, kick him in the nuts. Don't be shy. Kick him hard." She based this advice on all the serial killers—Ted Bundy, Angelo Buono, Kenneth Bianchi, etc.—who had used fake police badges to effortlessly subdue their victims ("A police badge isn't kryptonite, kid, for the sake of Christ on the cross," Flo insisted). This was in addition to the actual policemen who themselves turned out to be serial killers and/or rapists—Manuel Pardo,

Drew Peterson, Lawrence B. Woods, etc.—"and don't even get me started on the security guards," she would say. To Flo, security guards were all shady miscreants. "It's the perfect job for a killer on the lam," she maintained. No disrespect to the dead one at his desk behind us. But in any case, to hear Flo say she was ready to toss the towel to the authorities meant she was definitely out of ideas.

But I wasn't on the same page just yet. When we reached the mess of caskets, cadavers, and exploded innards we'd left behind the wheel of the L-1011, I gingerly stepped over the gory rubble to get a closer look at what was left of the guy who had exploded. It was not pretty. But at least the area above his shoulders suffered minimal impact. The fresher blood that covered his face from his internal combustion was a different color than the stain that spread over his chin and neck. That was because the latter wasn't a blood stain at all. It was a birthmark.

"I think you do know this guy," I said to Flo.

"I was just kidding when I said that." She sounded weary.

"I don't think so." I showed her the paper I'd taken from the bulletin board. It was a missing-person announcement. "Have You Seen John Lassateur?" it read.

Yes. I believe we had.

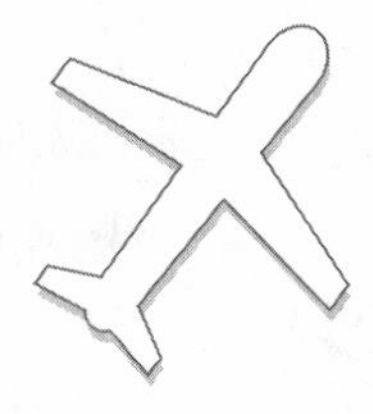

CHAPTER 13

"Holy Christ," Flo exclaimed. "What the hell happened to the poor guy?"

Before I could speculate, an employee bus came careening into the hangar. It was headed for us, then cut an extreme left, popped up on one side, plunked heavily back down onto four wheels, ran over the picnic table, and came to a stop by crashing into the security hut. In the distance I could barely make out the driver.

"Otis!" I screamed.

The door flew open and Otis descended onto the tarmac, waving to us gamely, only to have Hackman fly out from the bus and tackle him from behind. The two tumbled across the concrete in a dusty ball of kicking feet, flying fists, and curses. *Had they been fighting all this time?* I wondered. I picked up the crowbar and ran toward them to give Otis a hand. Flo, ever the pragmatist, had gone the opposite direction, unhooked the tug from the tow carts, hopped aboard, and pulled up alongside me before I'd reached halfway to the commotion. I hopped on and she sped us the rest of the way.

Hackman had Otis by the hair and was trying to knee him in the face, but Otis wriggled free and felled him with a kick to the back of the knee. Hackman, as swift as he was hefty, rolled over and was on his feet again in a second. The two of them made a curious sight—Otis with his black eye patch and Hackman with his mummy-bandaged arm, a result from when Flo slashed it before. Who knows what happened to the gun Hackman had earlier, or, for that matter, the body of the bus driver he'd shot with it.

I jumped from the tug and ran toward them with the crowbar raised in my hand, swinging wildly. I was so furious I discarded a few of Otis's six rules of hand-to-hand combat he'd taught me. Here is the list:

OTIS'S 6 RULES OF HAND-TO-HAND COMBAT

1. Be Aggressive.
2. Be Unrelenting.
3. Vary Your Attacks.
4. Use the Element of Surprise.
5. Disable or be Disabled.
6. Keep the Opponent in Your Sight.

The most important rules for my purpose in this instance were numbers five and six. Those rules I discarded.

I swung the crowbar at Hackman's head with all my strength, missed, and stumbled forward, barely having time to throw my arms forward to break my face-plant. Unfortunately it was the hand that held the crowbar, which sailed from my grip and scuttled across the ground to rest at the tip of Hackman's foot. Hackman swept it up as though he expected it to be there, swung it with all his might, and hit Otis square and solid on the blind side of his head, embedding the bent tip into his skull.

The sound of the crowbar hitting bone was sickening. Otis's face went instantly white, then gray, then his body crumpled and hit the ground like a bag of hammers. It was terrifying to see. Like that time on television when I watched a professional downhill skier wipe out on the slope during a competition, sending her body into a lateral spin right into one of the concrete snow barriers that bordered the ramp. In the instant her spinning body was deflected back onto the slope—that very instant—you knew she was dead. You did not have to take a pulse, check her pupils, watch for her breath, or do anything else you see people do to check for signs of life. You did not have to "shake and shout" as flight attendants were instructed during annual training in the event they encounter someone who is unresponsive. You saw the life leak out of her. You knew that girl was dead.

Flo threw herself on the ground at Otis's side. She placed his head in her lap and slapped his cheek. Shouting his name. "Wake up, you bastard!" she shrieked at him. Otis lay like a beached sea lion, motionless.

Hackman had retrieved the crowbar and stood bent at the waist, catching his breath, smiling smugly at Flo. He straightened and walked with purpose to stand above her. He raised the crowbar menacingly, and sneered, "Shut up, you stupid old . . ." but he didn't finish, because right then I put a bullet in his brain.

CHAPTER 14

I may have discarded numbers five and six of Otis's rules for hand-to-hand combat, but not number four, the element of surprise. While Hackman had been headed back for Otis, I'd run onto the bus and found the gun he'd used previously. It must have been lost earlier in their battle, and had to be resting under one of the seats along the driver's side, I knew, owing to the side wheelie Otis had popped on the way inside the hangar. Anything loose on the floor would have accumulated along the left side of the bus.

A look of surprise overtook the sneer on Hackman's face as the bullet entered his forehead. A small red dot appeared over his right eye, then grew larger and seemed to bubble up and pour out down his face. He dropped where he stood, grazing Flo's shoulder as he hit the ground. She kicked at him angrily.

I stumbled over and sat down next to her. "Give me that," she said, and I handed her the gun. Sirens blared in the distance as she continued to stroke Otis's forehead. I marveled at how relaxed his face seemed. The sound of sirens grew closer.

"Go," Flo instructed me. I couldn't just yet. "April, you just killed someone. You have to get." I knew she was right. If I stuck around until the police arrived it could be days before I'd be free to find Malcolm, and that's if the police believed a word I said, which they tended to be reluctant to do. There was also the problem that the only exit was through the front of the hangar, with nothing to hide behind for acres in each direction.

"Can't you come with me?" I pleaded.

"Someone's gotta serve as a witness and it can't be you. You're already wanted for one murder and here you are with another dead body." *Not to mention the pyramid of corpses on the other side of that airplane.*

She was right again, and urged me again to go, so I did. I ran toward the scaffolding, grabbed one of the lunch boxes on the way, climbed into the L-1011, and hid there, peeking out the galley window as the flashing lights and sirens got closer. When they arrived I saw an ambulance, a fire truck, and two company security vehicles. *Where are the police?* They must have been close behind. I heard the EMTs pronounce Otis dead, then load his body into the back of the ambulance. One of the security vehicles drove under the plane over to its starboard side. The galley didn't have a porthole on that side so I could only imagine their faces when they discovered the pile of desecrated caskets.

The other security officers tried to get Flo to go with them peacefully, but she kicked and cursed and hollered that the "real police" could find her at the hospital if they wanted to talk to her. I wasn't surprised, considering that her opinion of security guards was three notches below her opinion of police officers. ("They're all just thugs with toy badges," she liked to say, "no offense to Officer Ned.") She jumped into the ambulance and perched beside the stretcher. I did not find it comforting that they didn't sound their siren as they pulled out of the hangar and down the tarmac. No one had seen, or thought to look, inside the dark security hut where the guard lay dead. Perhaps it was because the bus had crashed into it and efforts were made to preserve the scene.

The firemen placed a call to the police, then left after the security guards assured them they'd wait for the police to arrive. I crawled through the hole in the bulkhead and concealed the opening behind me by parking a cart in front of it. I curled up in the forward cargo area, closed my eyes, and, incredibly, dozed off for a bit. Now that Hackman was dead I had a horrible ability to relax a little. I almost wished this wasn't true, like I should have been clutching my knees to my chest and keening like an undermedicated mental patient, but I guess your psyche can only take so much stress before it either breaks or takes things in stride.

This ability to keep from disintegrating under pressure is something airlines look for in their flight attendants, by the way, owing to all the crises that happen in the air. But no matter how skilled you think you are at recognizing this quality in a person, it's still kind of a crapshoot. Flo told me about how she once had to prepare a DC-9 for an emergency landing after the captain lost both engines after initial approach. There were two other flight attendants onboard that day, and one of them simply sat in the jumpseat the whole time, looking into a compact and applying lipstick.

"I tried to get her to get off her ass and help, but she was gone," Flo whistled and fluttered her fingers. "She mashed that lipstick to a nub, going over her lips with it over and over, like in a daze." If the plane had crashed she'd have made a pretty casualty but would have been useless evacuating the passengers to safety. Luckily the pilot was able to restart one of the engines on final approach. When the plane hit the runway, it caused just enough damage for the incident to be reported as a really "rough" landing, as opposed to a "crash" landing.

Flo, though, for all her blustering and crusty exterior, was exactly what any airline would hope for in a flight attendant. She'd seen everything during her decades in the air, and was surprised by little. Here is a short list of mortifications Flo has had to endure throughout her career:

1. The year Flo was hired, stewardesses were not allowed to be married, divorced, or even widowed. She told me of one coworker who, prior to her hiring, had been wed just a month when her husband was killed in Vietnam. When WorldAir found that out they canned her like a truckload of tuna.

2. It used to be mandatory for stewardesses to wear restrictive girdles under their uniforms. Supervisors commonly roamed the stew lounges pinching asses to ensure this requirement was being met.

3. Stews used to be subjected to a weight limit. This wasn't really a problem for Flo, who was as big as a baby carrot, but for people like my mother, for example, who was 5'7", and who had a weight limit of 132 pounds when she was hired—132 pounds was the *minimum* on the range of healthy weight for women of her height, yet it was the maximum she could weigh without getting fired.

4. Stews used to be forced to retire when they turned 30.

5. Stews used to have to wear heels two inches or higher to perform their duties. When an employee's duties include carrying unconscious passengers off the plane during emergencies, it was a bit stupefying why the attractiveness of her shoe ware would play a part, let alone a mandatory part.

So when you endure this kind of blatant objectification as a matter of daily course, evidently you become a very flexible person. When it came to the darkness of the human soul, and the dangers it caused, Flo seemed to question nothing and accept everything. "Ain't nobody coming in on a white horse to save your ass," she was fond of telling me, mostly while we were watching some reality-crime television program depicting the plight of some poor victim too terrified to do anything other than everything her attacker demanded. "You got to save your own ass."

She wasn't always this way. "I used to be a starry-eyed idiot just like any of these other girls," she indicated the television. "What happened?" I asked. "I wised up," she said, and left it at that. I personally think Flo turned out fine, and imagined that my father's mother, her best friend, would have turned out just like her if she'd lived. Flo and my grandmother met in the sixties during stewardess training. That was back when WorldAir crews worked trips to exotic locations like Morocco and Borneo, before the mass implementation in the eighties of "hub-and-spoke" route systems that genericized crew layovers for most major airlines. But until then, Flo and my grandmother traveled the globe together, and the world was their personal balloon on a string.

I had a picture of them taken in 1979, standing in the huge engine well of a 747. They were each wearing one of the iconic Pucci-designed pink-and-orange uniforms from back then, which consisted of a short tunic over hot pants and white patent-leather boots. Their bleached platinum hair was styled in the poofy cascade that was popular then, with a center strand clipped at the crown like Sharon Tate in the movie posters for *Valley of the Dolls.* Their beauty was radiant. My father was four years old then, having been born just two years after stewardesses won the right to have children and keep their jobs. Imagine fighting for the right to be a parent and employed. Male stewards were not subject to the same restrictions. My grandmother died the year after the picture was taken, from hypobaropathy, or altitude sickness, while climbing Mount Kilimanjaro with Flo and a group of fellow flight attendants on a ten-day layover in Tanzania.

I was startled awake by the sounds of more sirens. *How long had I been out?* Surely just minutes. I peeked out the porthole and saw that the police had arrived. "How do you turn the lights on in this place?" one shouted. The hangar was dark, thank God, otherwise I wouldn't have felt free to peek from above like I did, even though it was a distance of about 30 feet high. At present the police were trying to work with the minimal ambient light coming from the vending machines against the wall by the security hut, along with the headlights from the police cars. Uniformed officers cordoned off the area and began positioning floodlights around the crime scene. Plainclothes homicide detectives perused the area taking notes.

A police photographer began taking Polaroid shots of the crime scene before the others had finished with the network of lights. Contrary to popular belief, cops don't use chalk, tape, or anything else to outline the body at the scene of a homicide. It would contaminate the crime scene. Instead they rely on the photographs for reference after the body had been collected and sent to the morgue.

"Get those lights working," the detective shouted again. A forensic technician waved him off—the body wasn't going anywhere—and continued to unspool the anaconda of electrical cords with the objective of getting power to the portable lighting system. The photographer snapped away with the Polaroid, flooding the area with interludes of bright flashes. As the bulb illuminated the area where Hackman fell, something looked wrong. *Flash.* Darkness. *Flash. What is that?* Darkness.

Finally the technician found the outlet and plugged in the portable floodlight system. The hangar lit up like the surface of the sun, and I immediately saw clearly what had been bothering me about the crime scene. It was Hackman's head. Or lack thereof.

CHAPTER 15

Until now, LaVonda and Officer Ned had pretty much been sitting rapt during the last few hours, listening to me recount the previous day's events, as though I was telling them scary campfire stories or something. But then LaVonda jumped to her feet and began pacing the length of the cargo catwalk. "Oh, no you did NOT." She circled once, came back, and sat back down. "You did NOT just tell me Mr. Hackman's head went and walked off on its own. No, no, no siree, you did NOT." She got up again to perform the same curious pacing ritual. "I'm gettin' the chills," she shuddered.

For the last few hours the atmosphere had been peppered with bustling sounds coming from the hangar outside—the scaffolding removal, the change of shift of the police officers standing guard, the cleanup of the crime scene, etc.

"Sit down, LaVonda," Officer Ned whispered hoarsely, "and be quiet."

I remembered it was to the chagrin of the board members, and even that of Officer Ned, that LaVonda had taken her new job at WorldAir so seriously. Since the title had been invented specifically for her, there had yet to be any concise job description created or even a list of duties pertinent to the position. So LaVonda took it upon herself to create her own duties, which turned out to consist mainly of following Officer Ned's every move.

"You are not my assistant," Officer Ned tried to reason with her one day recently. "It's bad enough I have April here hanging out like this is the school cafeteria." I perked my head up from my iPad as I lay on his leather office couch surrounded by empty peanut packets. "I don't need you hovering around me all the time, too!"

"I am the WorldAir Trauma Liaison," LaVonda puffed her chest out proudly, "and it says right here in my job description that my duties include . . . April, what's a fancy way of saying 'stick close by'?"

"'Keep in close proximity to,'" I answered.

"Right, my duties include keeping in close proximity to the head of security, and that is you."

"You just typed that into your iPad right now while we were sitting here!" Officer Ned hollered.

"So?" LaVonda made a flourish as she pressed the "save" button. "There, it's official. Now don't be tellin' me how to do my job."

"It actually makes sense," I piped in. "If she sticks around you long enough she's bound to run into someone who's been traumatized."

I knew Officer Ned would throw himself into an active volcano for my sake if he had to, and he'd probably do the same for LaVonda, too. All that blustering and hollering was just a facade to keep people from getting close. And you can hardly blame him. Look what happened the minute he took me under his wing: Two bullets to the torso, that's what. But like I said earlier, he looks to have healed nicely.

Today, LaVonda was resolute in the power of support dogs to allay trauma. She hugged Beefheart to her chest and said, "Okay, I feel better now."

I focused back on the subject at hand. "Hackman's head didn't walk off on its own," I said. "Someone took it."

"Why would someone steal a dead man's head?"

Didn't we all want to know that. I asked Officer Ned if he had the chance to talk to the investigators about the contents of the disrupted caskets that were also found at the crime scene. He looked at me with furrowed brow.

"April, there weren't any caskets here when the police arrived," he said. "And, believe me, I looked around the area before I climbed up here. I didn't see any evidence of exploded corpses."

"Are you saying you don't believe me?" I was incredulous. "What do you call this?" I pointed to a small Rorschach pattern of specks below the knees of my cargo pants. I regretted having scrubbed at them with the pile of alcohol swabs I'd found in the first-aid kit the night before.

"That doesn't look like human remains to me, April," he answered worriedly. "Listen, are you sure you're feeling okay?"

"How do you know what exploded gizzards look like?" LaVonda defended me. "Look at this poor child! She's been crashed up, burned up, beat up, and thoroughly messed up in the last twenty-four hours. Look at that bruise on her forehead! She needs our help."

"LaVonda, we talked about this, remember?" Officer Ned chastised her. *They talked about this?* "Remember your training."

"I'm just sayin'," she mumbled. "It could have happened like she said."

"LaVonda, please focus, the doctor said the delusions can be quite convincing," Officer Ned said.

"What doctor?" I panicked.

"April, you cracked your head pretty hard on the asphalt after falling off the bus, right? I saw the footage on YouTube." Damn the advent of social media.

"This is not about me hitting my head!" I protested. "I didn't hallucinate all this! It happened just like I told you!" Officer Ned reached out to put a caring touch on my forehead, and I smacked his hand away. "What about the dead guard in the security hut? Huh? I can't conjure a dead security guard out of my imagination."

"April, there was no dead guard in the security hut," he informed me. I looked at him agog. He continued, "I talked to the actual guard who was there, or who was supposed to have been there, but he'd stepped out to use the can, and when he came back he found Hackman. He's the one who called the police."

I shook my head. "No, that's not right." I looked at LaVonda imploringly. "That's not right, is it, LaVonda?"

She didn't say anything, instead she handed me back Captain Beefheart. "Honey child, I think you've been traumatized."

"Hell yes, I've been traumatized! Haven't you heard a single word I said?"

LaVonda looked pained before saying, "I heard every word you said."

"Don't you believe me?"

Officer Ned interrupted, "April, we just want to do what's best and make sure you're getting the care you need."

"What about Flo?" I brightened. "Have you spoken with Flo? She'll tell you everything."

"Ah, April," Officer Ned continued cautiously, "we did call Flo and she said she hasn't seen you since the day before yesterday."

I guffawed incredulously. "She did not say that. Call her again, right now. Call her. And use her work cell," I added, remembering her personal cellphone lay broken up somewhere off GA400.

Officer Ned did as I asked and put the phone on speaker. Flo picked up on the first ring. "What?" she groused. Officer Ned asked her to do him a favor and confirm once again where she was the night before. "I was right here, Thor, how many times you want me to say it? I was here all night drinking vodka and watching *MacGyver* DVDs. Same thing I do every night."

"I think we have a bad connection," Officer Ned complained to her. "What's that sound?"

"That's just me," Flo said. "Tabasco sauce is getting low, I gotta smack it outta the bottle"—*smack smack smack.* "You can't make a Bloody Mary without Tabasco sauce."

"Okay, so you were home last night?"

"Tell the truth," I implored her.

"Is that Crash?" Flo's voice brightened. *Smack, smack, smack.* "Tell her I said to keep kicking ass." He handed the phone to me.

"Flo, the truth," I begged.

"I'm telling the truth, kid," she chuckled. *Smack smack smack.* "I was right here, watching *MacGyver.* Season four, episode eleven." Officer Ned gently took the phone from my hand, thanked Flo, and hung up.

He eyed me expectantly. LaVonda looked on guiltily. "This is harder than I thought it would be," she mumbled.

"April, please, it's better that you come with me." He held his hand out to me. "Otherwise I'll have to tell them where you are and they'll have to come here to get you. If that happens I can't guarantee things will go smoothly." I held Beefheart close to me and backed away from him down the catwalk toward the avionics area. Officer Ned followed me, and LaVonda after him.

"Excuse me, Thor," LaVonda interjected. Officer Ned winced at the nickname. Only two people on earth were allowed to use it: Flo, who called all tall, muscular men "Thor," and LaVonda, who had been introduced to him through Flo as such. "But I did not sign up for this," LaVonda continued. "You didn't say anything about us throwing her over to the police like a bloody piece of meat. I'm here 'cause she in distress. She need medical attention."

Exasperated, Officer Ned turned to her. "Oh my God! You believe her, don't you? This is exactly what the doctor warned us about. She's suffering from a TBI, LaVonda! Her delusions are going to be very persuasive, but we have to stand strong. If she doesn't get the help she needs she could suffer permanent brain damage. And if she doesn't go with us willingly, what choice do we have but to call the police? Get your head back in the game and focus."

"Don't tell me where to put my head," she argued. "I know where my head needs to be, and just because some doctor—"

"Who is this doctor?" I cried.

"—waved around a bunch of papers, some high-falutin' FBI forensic psychologist, came into our office—"

"*My* office," Officer Ned said.

"—talkin' about how our sweet April here is suffering from some 'psychotic episode' and going around killin' people—"

"What?" I cried.

"—don't mean we should roll over like a coupla hobos and let them have at her. She needs a lawyer, for one."

"What she needs," Officer Ned pointed at me with his arm outstretched, then looked back at LaVonda, "is a hospital."

I reached into my back pocket and grabbed the handcuffs I'd picked off my wrists the night before. Before Officer Ned could react, I'd clicked a bracket around his outstretched wrist and locked the other one around the metal shelving grid supporting the avionics area.

At first he seemed disbelieving, tentatively shaking his arm like the cuff was a party favor that could break easily. Then the realization set in and he yanked his arm around more furiously. "April, give me the keys to these immediately. This isn't funny." I shook my head. "The keys," he insisted. I shook my head again.

"Oh, girl, you did NOT just handcuff Thor to the airplane," howled LaVonda. "I swear to Lord Jesus Christ on the cross, you did NOT do that." She threw her arms above her head and paced up and down the catwalk, slapping her thighs and howling with laughter.

"April," Officer Ned growled. "Unlock me this instant."

I backed away from him and handed Beefheart to LaVonda, who calmed down to a few snorts and the wiping of tears. "Yeah, child, you gonna unlock him, right?"

"I don't have a key," I said. Officer Ned began yanking his arm in earnest now, and LaVonda lapsed into another laughing fit. I begged them to be quiet. "Just listen to what I have to say, please," I implored. LaVonda covered her mouth and Officer Ned stilled himself into a solid wall of muscle and rage, glaring at me.

"I'm sorry, Officer Ned," I began, "but you have to listen to me. Flo said she was home last night, alone, *like every night.* Think about that."

Officer Ned should have known as well as I did that Flo had a flourishing social life, having stayed friends with all her ex-husbands and ex-boyfriends as well as all their new partners, who were constantly, to mixed success, setting her up with someone new. She lived next to the airport in Hapeville and hung out at a bar called the Bricklayer's Arms, where the owners liked her so much they allowed her to get behind the bar and mix her own cocktails.

"She said she was watching *MacGyver* DVDs," he countered.

"Flo mostly watches *MacGyver* on a portable DVD player while sitting in a jumpseat at work," I reminded him. It was a pastime that violated a strict rule of employment at WorldAir. In fact, it was a miracle she hadn't been busted by the cellphone camera of a disgruntled passenger, but Flo had a way with disgruntled passengers. It was a skill born from 47 years in the passenger-service industry; if you can't keep passengers satisfied, at least keep them laughing. No one ever complained about her, or at least not that anyone knew about, as the person in charge of assessing WorldAir passenger complaints was also one of Flo's ex-boyfriends.

But back to the point—yeah, the thought of Flo sitting at home alone belting hooch and watching reruns was ridiculous. Surely Officer Ned could see that.

He frowned and seemed to think about it, then shook it off. "April, don't you see you're acting crazy? Look at this." He shook his handcuffed arm at me. "You're deluded, suffering the textbook symptoms of a traumatic brain injury. LaVonda, tell her . . . wait, where's LaVonda."

Click. LaVonda slapped another set of cuffs on his free hand and then fastened the other end to another part of the metal shelving grid. The effect had him splayed, like a big, handsome, black Fay Wray, across the bolted-down metal structure. LaVonda stepped away to escape his kicking legs, her eyes wide.

"I can't believe I just did that," she said.

"LaVonda, April, I'm serious, let me loose or there'll be hell to pay," Officer Ned roared, then calmed down, deciding on a different tack. "Okay, girls, heh, heh, joke's over. This has been really funny. LaVonda, where the hell did you even get your hands on a set of handcuffs?"

"You keep a pair in the top drawer of your desk," LaVonda said.

"These are my handcuffs?" he seethed.

"They're my handcuffs," LaVonda corrected. "I had them commissioned from HR. If you get a pair, I get a pair, it says so in my job description." At that, Officer Ned forgot about his new tack and became furious again, devolving into a mess of futile attempts to lunge at us. Finally he calmed once more.

"April, I will give you one minute to release me and we'll forget this ever happened," he tried to reason. "It's not your fault. You're suffering a psychotic lapse. And you," he looked at LaVonda, "you're suffering from Stockholm Syndrome."

"Stock-*what*?" LaVonda said skeptically.

I was impressed that Officer Ned had taken his airline-security training to heart. The syndrome to which he was referring was named after an incident in Stockholm in the seventies, when a number of hostages were held captive in a bank vault during a robbery. Over time the hostages began to side with the robber, and even eschewed help from the police. After the situation was neutralized, many of the hostages even testified for the defense.

Today, airline inflight personnel are annually versed on this and other hostage-related syndromes in their training exercises. Should a hijacking occur, this knowledge would come in handy. But I was not hijacking a plane. I was just trying to find my friend Malcolm.

"Hear me out, please," I asked them. Officer Ned remained silent while LaVonda nodded her head and gestured for me to continue. "Flo mentioned *MacGyver* episode eleven, season four," I began, "and you know I know all the episodes by heart, right?" A moot point; Flo had gotten them both hooked on the reruns as well. "In that episode, the plot involved two criminals talking on a tapped phone. Got that? *A tapped phone.*"

LaVonda nodded her head enthusiastically, but it was Officer Ned I needed to convince. I could see indecision begin to soften the features of his face.

"Right!" LaVonda chimed in to move things along. "That's what all that slapping sound was, right?" I had to love LaVonda. She was looking for anything to back the fact that—by siding with me—she'd gone with her intuition above her training. And the fact is that there were many ways to tell your phone had been tapped, and I'm sure Flo knew most of them, as she was privy as I was to Otis's list of five warning signs that your phone is being tapped. Here is the list:

OTIS'S LIST OF 5 WARNING SIGNS THAT YOUR PHONE IS BEING TAPPED

1. **Overheating.** It is normal for a cellphone to generate heat when you're using it—a result of the battery being active—but if your cell seems really hot even when you're not using it, your line may have been compromised.

2. **A Drained Battery.** A tapped phone loses its battery life faster than a normal phone because it's constantly recording conversations, even when it appears to be sitting idle.
3. **A Controlling Romantic Partner.** It's now easier than ever for stalkers to tap someone's phone, with devices like spy SIM-card readers easily available to the public. These devices can be used to remotely check the deleted messages and phone activity of nearly any phone of your choosing.
4. **Static.** If you hear static, not just when you are on a call, but when you are *not* using your cellphone, it's a sign your phone is tapped. Listen for a pulsating static, as opposed to simple bad reception. Static with a regular pulse indicates someone on another end switching back and forth between lines.
5. **Weird Cellphone Activity.** If your phone spontaneously shuts down, lights up, installs programs, or otherwise acts like it's possessed by a poltergeist, that's an indication that it's tapped and controlled by someone else.

The thought of Uncle Otis brought the sting of tears to my eyes again, but I fought them back. The last thing he would have wanted was for my mind to be clouded and diverted from my mission by sorrowful thoughts about him. So back to Flo's phone; the sound in her connection indicated none of these things on Otis's list. Instead it was simply a deliberate *slap, slap, slapping* that Flo said she was creating herself. Perhaps she was just making herself a Bloody Mary after all, but I had a very different opinion.

"No, that sound wasn't a wire tap," I surmised. "It was Morse code. Three episodes of three."

"What's it mean?" LaVonda exhaled in wonderment.

Officer Ned was the first to answer. "It means S.O.S.," he said, "the international signal for distress." He shook his arms vigorously. "Now get me the hell out of these cuffs."

After he assured me he wouldn't hogtie me and drag me off to the authorities, I took the picks from my pocket and went to work on one set of handcuffs. LaVonda was more hesitant. "You sure you're not mad at me?" she asked.

"I'm furious at you," he answered. "But I'll wait until all this is over with before I fire you."

"You can't fire me, it says so in my job description," she huffed, unhooking her massive janitor ring. She tried hit-and-miss to find the correct key by attempting to insert each one into the lock like Prince Charming looking for the foot to fit the glass slipper. In the end it was quicker for me to just pick her lock as well, and soon Officer Ned was free, rubbing his wrists and looking undecided on whether to reprimand us or galvanize us into action. Finally he squared his shoulders and seemed about to dispense direction on our next step, when suddenly all three of us stumbled and fell. Captain Beefheart went skittering from LaVonda's arms down the catwalk, where he touched the bulkhead like it was home base and came skipping back to us with eyes excited and tongue lolling.

"What happened?" LaVonda cried. "Who moved the floor?"

"Shhhh!" I whispered. "The floor isn't moving. The *plane* is moving."

"Oh, Lord, this plane is NOT moving. No, it is NOT." She sat upright and shook her head. But the plane *was* moving. I pulled the pairing summary from my pocket and realized we were within three hours of the aircraft's scheduled takeoff for

Grand Cayman. A mechanic must have been dispatched to tow the vessel to the gate in preparation for departure, which explained the lack of engine noise.

"NOT moving. NOT moving," LaVonda keened.

"Be quiet, please," Officer Ned told her. He stood and, since there were no guard rails along in this part of the cargo area to steady him, he kind of crab-walked to the bulkhead, where he pushed the meal cart aside and made his way through the hole and into the galley. The officer guarding the hangar must have forgotten to tell his replacement that LaVonda and Officer Ned were inside the aircraft. Maybe he didn't think it was necessary, seeing as how the two of them were airline employees and this here plane was a big chunk of the airline itself. The hangar was so huge that the aircraft was not considered part of the crime scene below, because it would have been like cordoning off the top half of an office building because a murder had been committed in its parking lot.

LaVonda appeared behind us, clutching Beefheart, steadying herself against the galley counter. She closed her eyes and began to pray under her breath.

"What's wrong?" I asked her.

"I ain't never flown in a plane before."

CHAPTER 16

"LaVonda," Officer Ned said. "We're not flying, we're just getting towed to the gate. From there you can take the jetway back to the concourse."

She exhaled and seemed to relax, though any tiny jostle of the airplane made her tense up again. I smiled in spite of the circumstances. Who knew LaVonda was afraid to fly? I never bothered to ask her. When she moved to Atlanta from Los Angeles last year, LaVonda had driven the moving truck while her partner flew over with their two children. Now here was a woman who was afraid to fly employed as an airline trauma liaison to help with people who were afraid to fly. It made a strange kind of sense, if you asked me.

As I said earlier, the Atlanta International Airport covered about 133 square miles. So it would take a good while for us to get to the gate. Officer Ned banged his phone against the palm of his hand when he realized the battery had gone dead. He asked to borrow LaVonda's, but she'd left hers on the electrical cart she'd used to drive over to the hangar. "Do you at least have a charger?" he asked.

"Of course I have a charger." She produced it from her vest with a flourish. "For what good it does. There's no outlet here." She was partially right. There were plenty of outlets in the galley along the power strip above the meal-cart bays, but they were the 30-amp, four-prong kind. On top of that, the power to them had probably been cut long ago, as most domestic flights don't offer hot food anymore. And to further stack cards against us, LaVonda's charger was the kind you plug into car cigarette lighters, not the outlet kind. Unfortunately it was useless. Officer Ned thanked-but-no-thanked her and she tucked the cord back in her pocket.

I led LaVonda to one of the jumpseats on the side of the dumbwaiter elevators at the rear of the small galley, and buckled her in. We were only traveling at a moderate taxi along the tarmac, but she seemed set to panic nonetheless. I tucked Captain Beefheart in her lap, which comforted her. Captain Beefheart was not only a smart dog, but mellow as a monk. I can count on one hand how many times I'd heard him bark at—let alone bite—anyone. Since the crash last year, he'd become somewhat of an Internet celebrity, thanks in large part to Flo's JetHag Facebook page, which each Thursday featured an update devoted to Captain Beefheart. These updates often took the form of lists, such as "Captain Beefheart's 15 Best Selfies," or "Captain Beefheart's Top 10 Air-Travel Safety Tips," or my favorite, "Captain Beefheart's 5 Ways to Survive an Aircraft Fire." Here is that list:

CAPTAIN BEEFHEART'S 5 WAYS TO SURVIVE AN AIRCRAFT FIRE

1. **Don't drink alcohol.** Airline studies have proven that a majority of people who don't make it out of a burning fuselage have alcohol in their systems. So don't order alcohol during the beverage service. (I'm almost positive Flo invented this statistic to lower her workload on her own scheduled flights. But still it probably wasn't bad advice to caution against being drunk during an emergency.)
2. **Keep your head at armrest level while crawling out of the smoke-filled cabin.** (While smoke rises, poisonous industrial fumes sink, so the most breathable air would be located in between.)
3. **Before takeoff, count the rows to your nearest exit.** (Most likely you'll be blinded by smoke and need to feel your way off the aircraft.)
4. **Even if they drop from the ceiling (which they probably will) don't use the oxygen masks during a fire.** (Pure oxygen is highly flammable, so bypass the masks if you don't want to combust before the fireball even reaches you.)
5. **Request an exit-row seat.** (Seriously, all that speculation about which seats of the aircraft are safer in the event of a crash—front, mid, aft—is useless. The safest seats on any aircraft are those located by the exits. The sooner off the airplane the better your chances of surviving.)

Maybe I had an affinity for this list because my own father—my real father, not that spineless asstard Ash Manning—died in an aircraft fire when I was four years old. I still remember how he used to wake me up each morning. He'd put his hand on my face and wait for me to smile. "Hi, Goldie," he'd say. That was his nickname for me, Goldie, on account of how in the summertime the color of my hair almost matched the color of my skin. No one else ever called me that anymore, and I missed it. I liked it so much better than "Crash."

"Time to open your eyes." My father would shake me gently, then a tad more firmly. "Time to wake up."

He did not follow Beefheart's five steps. No, instead he ran *away* from the exit to assist some passengers in the back of the plane whose evacuation was being obstructed—and that wrong step cost him his life. The fuel in the wings ignited and the plane was engulfed before the firemen could unroll their hoses. Anyone who didn't make it out by then didn't make it at all.

There should be a sixth step in Beefheart's list, and that would be "Leave Everything," because the obstruction impeding the evacuation that day—the one responsible for my father's death and those of two other people—was a passenger attempting to retrieve his bag from the overhead bin.

LaVonda thanked me for buckling her in, then sat there bug-eyed with worry, clutching Beefheart like he was a flotation device. I smiled out of endearment. "Don't worry," I told her, "we'll be at the jetway soon." She nodded wanly. Officer Ned, for his part, kept smacking his cellphone against his palm like he was trying to awaken a weary prizefighter. I wondered what phone call he had to make that was so pressing.

I pulled myself through the galley's ceiling hatch and up to the passenger area above so I could get a better vantage of our surroundings. The area below only afforded a single tiny window located in the galley door off the port side of the plane, which severely limited my lookout ability. I knew the L-1011 was empty because the scaffolding leading to the left-front entry door, the only door used during repairs and inspections, had been dissembled long ago. Besides, we would have heard anyone ambling aboard. An L-1011, while the engines are turned off, has all the sound insulation of a slumlord apartment building.

Eventually we came to a stop way outside one of the domestic concourses. I assumed we were waiting to pull up to a gate, as all of them appeared to be full with other aircraft connected to the concourse by a collection of jetways, which extended from the concourse like flexible, biomorphic tubes atop adjustable metal support pillars on wheels. But then I felt our aircraft jostle as the tow tug unhooked itself from the nose, and saw the tug drive off into the distance, leaving us stranded in a remote area of the tarmac.

"Where we at?" I heard LaVonda exclaim from the galley below. "They hook up the jetway yet?"

"Not yet." I tried to sound reassuring as I hopped back through the hatch, dropping to my feet in front of her jumpseat. "Hold tight."

"Hold tight? What the hell do you think I'm doing? Hold tight. Right. Me and Beefy are strapped the hell in," she said nervously. "Excuse my mouth. I tend to use the word 'hell' a lot when I'm having the hell scared out of me."

I saw that she'd tucked Beefheart against her chest under one of her shoulder straps. Out of habit I instructed her to take him out. It's never safe to strap a baby in under a seatbelt with you. The centrifugal force from an impact will crush it between your body and the restraint, I explained. "Oh, don't talk like that," she begged me, removing Beefheart from under her belt. "I did

NOT hear you say the words 'impact' and 'crushed' right now. No I did NOT."

I informed Officer Ned of our location on the tarmac, and he sighed with resignation. "That's why I've been trying to pull up my cell," he said. "I was afraid they'd do this."

"Do what?" LaVonda asked.

"Use a remote gate," he answered.

"What the hell is a remote gate?"

"It's when they park the plane off the concourse and bus the passengers over," I smacked my forehead. *Of course* they'd use a remote gate! Why waste an expensive passenger gate and jetway for a ferried flight containing only crew members and nonrevenue corporate wanks? Why didn't I think of this? I wondered if I wasn't suffering from brain trauma after all.

"What? What does this mean?" LaVonda looked from me to Officer Ned and back again.

"Ah, it just means, you know," Officer Ned spoke evenly, patting her hand to allay her alarm, "that we might have to go along for the ride."

"What ride? I ain't up for no ride! This has been ride enough! What ride?"

Eventually she lapsed into a daze, staring straight ahead. Officer Ned snapped his fingers near her face a few times, but it didn't register even an eye blink. Finally we left her like that. She was strapped into the jumpseat and probably didn't know how to extricate herself, which precluded her from jumping up and performing her signature "Hooting Panic Pacing" up and down the galley floor. So we left her there like that while we discussed this turn of events.

"What about Flo?" I asked. She had sent us a distress signal, after all.

Officer Ned furrowed his brow. He was worried about her as well. "Should you and LaVonda just drop to the tarmac and walk back?" Officer Ned asked me, but knew before I could answer that it wasn't a reasonable option. Not only was the belly of the airplane two stories above ground, but we were in a remote section of the runway in the middle of an expanse of flat tarmac. To leave the plane secretly would be impossible, as there was nothing to conceal our escape. Also, we would be taking our lives into our own hands, seeing as how we'd be potential airplane road kill by trying to navigate our way to the concourse surrounded by active runways.

"Maybe we could chance it anyway," he suggested.

"You can, but I'm not going anywhere." I was resolute. I'd known since I snatched the pairing summary from the printer in the guard house the night before; I was going to Grand Cayman. I didn't know exactly what this flight had to do with Malcolm's disappearance, but I knew it had something to do with it, and I was determined to find out.

"If Crash ain't getting off the plane," LaVonda finally snapped out of her bug-eyed fugue, "then I ain't either."

Officer Ned stamped his foot and yelled at us, to no effect. I was not to be deterred from my mission, and LaVonda was not to be deterred from my side. Finally Officer Ned resolved that, short of tossing us out the door and onto the tarmac—which, if it didn't kill us, certainly would have brought attention to our position and blown our cover—he determined to wait until the pilots boarded the aircraft to activate the engines and flight deck, then he could radio the police and request a "welfare visit" to Flo's place. But from this point forward we—LaVonda and I—were to keep ourselves safe and leave any confrontation with killers and/or criminals to him, he insisted. "I will seriously lose it if anything happens to either of you, or to Captain Beefheart for that matter. Don't test me, please."

He stopped ranting for a second to catch his breath, and was about to begin again when the galley door flew open, barely missing Officer Ned's head as it swung up to rest flush against the curve of the ceiling. Suddenly the galley was awash in the sound of jet engines and the voices of the ramp workers who had just pulled up to park a portable baggage conveyor at the mouth of the galley opening. Officer Ned and I ran back and secluded ourselves on the other side of the hole in the bulkhead. LaVonda, who remained strapped into the jumpseat, was concealed—barely—by the protrusion of the tiny elevator bay between her and the galley door. She sat stiffly upright with her lips firmly zipped, staring back at us from her seat. Beefheart wagged his tail, calmly and quietly, in her lap.

A WorldAir ramp worker jumped into the galley and gave a thumbs up to his colleague below, oblivious to our presence. Lord, I thought, we really need to train our employees better. For security reasons, employees are supposed to perform a "visual sweep" whenever they enter an aircraft to begin their duties. This guy did not even give the galley a cursory once-over. I heard the luggage conveyor crank up, and soon a travel casket emerged at the top and emptied into the galley, where the ramp worker pulled it aside to make room for the next one, and then the next, and so on until four travel caskets in stacks of two crowded the galley in the small space between the meal carts on either side. The ramp worker quickly secured the cargo against the floor ballast with a series of straps and ratchets, then hopped out and down the conveyor to join his colleague. They closed the door and drove away.

"What the hell is that?" LaVonda harped, pointing to the crates. She placed Beefheart on the floor and moved to unbuckle herself from the jumpseat. But a jumpseat harness is different from a regular car seatbelt, or even from the belts on the passenger seats above us. She pulled and tugged, but only managed to tighten her restraints. "What the hell? Get me outta here."

I gripped the center circular latch and turned it counterclockwise, and all the straps unfastened and fell away from LaVonda like the tentacles of an octopus that had suddenly grown very tired. She huffed and extricated herself from the inert straps. "I said what the hell is that?"

"Those are nothing," I tried to redirect her attention by calling to Captain Beefheart, who had crawled to the top of one of the stacks of crates.

"Those are not nothing," she countered me.

Officer Ned put his hand on her shoulder and told her to calm down, which is the exact opposite of what you should do to someone who needs to calm down. It even says in the flight attendant onboard manual to, quote, "Never use the words 'calm down' to a panicked or belligerent passenger." Instead we were to talk to them in even tones, validate their concerns, and lie our asses off to them that everything would be all right. Seriously, for some reason telling people to calm down always seems to make them freak out even more. LaVonda raised her voice, "Don't tell me to calm down. Just tell me what those are!"

Before I could tell him to lie to her, Officer Ned rolled his eyes in exasperation and said, "They're just human remains."

At that, LaVonda ran the width of the galley, touched the wall, and ran back again, her arms waving above her head. "Oh no you did NOT just tell me they's four dead bodies—oh, my GOD, I am NOT trapped in a plane with a bunch of dead bodies. I am NOT!"

Officer Ned kept telling her to calm down, and I kept telling him to stop telling her to calm down because it was making her panic even more, when suddenly our attention was drawn to Beefheart, who began barking. All of us fell silent to look at the little dog, dumbfounded. Beefheart, *barking*?

"Come here, sweet Beefy," LaVonda called to him. He ran toward her outstretched arms, only to touch her leg with his paw, double back, touch the casket, double back, touch her leg, etc. "Great, looks like you trained him to do your 'back-and-forth' fear dance," Officer Ned rolled his eyes, but I saw it differently. Finally Beefheart, secure that he'd gotten our attention, began scratching furtively at one of the bottom caskets.

"Help me open this up," I instructed the two of them. Officer Ned loosened the ratchets while I pulled the straps free. LaVonda joined in in spite of herself, mumbling, "You did NOT just say we gonna open a coffin."

Once the straps were free, we tried gently pushing the top casket off the bottom one, only despite our efforts it fell clumsily to the floor on its side and busted open. Christ, I thought, what do they make these things out of, Popsicle sticks? Out rolled a body encased in a large clear plastic bag. LaVonda looked away.

"She's wearing a WorldAir uniform," Officer Ned said of the diminutive corpse. Yes, it was true, and now I knew what happened to the bus driver that Hackman had shot in the face the night before.

Captain Beefheart continued to whimper and scratch at the next coffin. Funny, I thought, why this one and not the others? Officer Ned had taken one of the keys off LaVonda's monster key ring and was trying to pry open the lid. The process was as effective as attempting to open a soup can with a sewing needle, so I got up, returned to my hiding place behind the bulkhead, and came back with the crowbar I'd taken with me after my altercation with Mr. Hackman the night before. Deftly I pried the lid so it was loose enough for us to push open.

"How'd you get so good at that?" Officer Ned said.

"Don't ask."

The three of us put our palms against the lid and pushed it up and over until it hung open like . . . well, like a coffin lid. I looked inside the crate, and this time it was me who turned away. LaVonda put her arms around me and hugged me from behind. "You be strong," she whispered.

"Damn it. God *damn* it," Officer Ned cursed under his breath.

Inside the casket lay Uncle Otis. I took LaVonda's advice to be strong and turned back around. He was encased in plastic, still wearing the clothes I'd last seen him in, when Hackman had delivered that devastating blow to his skull. I fought back tears as I assessed the wound on the side of his head, next to the black patch over his left eye. A small speckle of blood in his blond locks was the only thing betraying the fatal blow. Captain Beefheart jumped into the casket and began licking the dead man's face through the loose plastic. My heart ached. Like Officer Ned, Beefheart always had an affection for Otis, probably because the man had been a mongrel in his own way.

"Oh, Sweet Beefcakes, stop that now," La Vonda gently admonished. "Come on, now, you are not licking a dead man's face. No, you are not."

Suddenly Otis's good eye shot open and gaped dead ahead. The three of us gasped and stumbled backward. What the hell? I thought. I'd heard of corpses doing all kinds of crazy things after death. In fact, there's an entire television show dedicated to crazy autopsy stories alone, narrated by the medical examiners themselves. Flo and my mother were addicted to it, and I had to admit I found it fascinating, too. Like how back in the day coroners used to tie bells to the fingers of the cadavers in case anyone was accidentally declared dead. Or the details about the sounds the corpses commonly made in the hours, even days, after death, such as sighs and coughs and gargle noises. You'd be surprised at how active dead people can be. Some even suddenly sit bolt upright on the coroner's slab, evidently a result of the combination of rigor mortis and the release of trapped gasses.

Suddenly Otis's body sat bolt upright in the casket.

LaVonda screamed and ran through the galley, through the bulkhead and into the forward cargo area, where she pounded against the cockpit floor hatch, yelling, "Lord Jesus Christ on the cross, there's a zombie! Let me out!"

Officer Ned looked frightened as well, and stepped between me and the casket, his arm out protectively. I peeked out from behind him and gaped at Otis in alarm. He still looked dead, his eye open but unseeing through the thick loose plastic, his arms limp and his back stiff.

"Beefheart, come here, pup," Officer Ned uneasily tried to whistle the dog away from the body, but in vain. Beefheart continued to yip, jumping up from Otis's lap, trying to lick the dead man's face. LaVonda continued to scream from behind the bulkhead.

Otis's corpse let out a sigh. Officer Ned jumped like a nervous cat and backed us farther away from the casket. Oh, Christ, I thought, is his body going to run the entire gamut of post mortem acrobatics? "Come on now, Beefheart." Officer Ned began to sound frantic. "Leave the dead man alone."

"What dead man?" Otis asked.

CHAPTER 17

Officer Ned buckled to his knees in a half faint. LaVonda's screams descended into unintelligible wailings. I flew forward, pulled the loose plastic away, and threw my arms around the man. "Uncle Otis!" I cried. "You're alive!"

"That's debatable," he coughed.

Officer Ned gathered himself and helped me help Otis stand. He climbed stiffly out of the crate and sat down on the floor. We sat down with him. LaVonda stopped howling and timidly peeked through the bulkhead at us. "You are NOT sitting there with a zombie, no you are NOT," she whimpered. Beefheart wriggled around in circles, a canine happy dance.

"Ouch," Otis rubbed his temple. "What happened?"

He was asking *us*? The last time I saw him he had a crowbar embedded in his head! "Uncle Otis, I thought you were dead! I saw Hackman bash in your head! You dropped like a shot moose!"

"That explains the migraine," he said. I got up and examined his head more closely. Dried blood crusted in his hair. "Ow, ouch, ow," he objected. I found the wound and gently pressed my thumb against it. Otis pushed my hand away, but I slapped his wrist and continued.

"What the hell is that?" I asked. I felt a pronounced dent in his head, but no pliable mealy-ness that would indicate a cranial fracture. I was also alarmed at the lack of blood in the area of the wound. "Do you have a head made of concrete?"

"Metal," he corrected me. "Or at least that part of my head is metal."

"You have a metal plate in your skull?" Officer Ned asked.

Of course Otis had a metal plate in his skull! He'd survived the most horrific aviation disaster in human history—and not without extensive injury.

"Yep," Otis concurred, "titanium plate in the head, titanium shoulder socket, titanium elbow joint. I'm pretty much a bionic man."

"Ooh, my second cousin Lamar had a metal plate in his skull." LaVonda's fear had turned into fascination as she stepped back through the bulkhead and over to Otis. She put her hand out to touch his head but he smacked it away. LaVonda was unperturbed. "Lamar got it after a building fell on his head during an earthquake in El Segundo. Afterward he said he couldn't see the color yellow anymore. He wasn't color blind, he was just yellow blind.

"Can you see the color yellow?" she asked Otis.

"I don't know, show me something yellow," he said.

I admit I was curious, too, but LaVonda couldn't find anything yellow to wave in front of his good eye to prove her theory. Officer Ned soon lost patience and asked us to get serious. "Otis, you don't remember being put in the travel casket?"

Otis shook his head, and for the first time seemed to notice the travel caskets. He cursed under his breath when he saw the lifeless body of his friend the bus driver. I felt bad for him; the two of them did seem to have a pleasant repartee. The claim sticker on her crate indicated this very flight to Grand Cayman, as did Otis's crate.

"Well, there's only one next step as I see it," he said, rising shakily to his feet. Officer Ned seemed to have the same idea. They both approached the other stack of caskets and pried the lid off the one on top. Inside was the guard from the security hut that Flo and I had found dead at his desk the night before.

"See?" LaVonda told Officer Ned. She was quickly getting accustomed to dead bodies. "April wasn't hallucinating after all."

"I gathered that," Officer Ned said grimly.

Otis and Officer Ned placed the lid back on the casket, lifted it, and set it aside so they could access the one underneath. I recognized this travel casket from the night before. It was the one we didn't open. At the time I didn't think it was necessary because it had come from Jacksonville. Surely some of these caskets had to be at the airport for non-nefarious reasons. Take the one containing the body of the middle-aged lady who broke my fall from the luggage conveyor. She was obviously on her way home after croaking on vacation or something. Here, this casket, in addition to the claim sticker with the GCM destination, still retained its original sticker showing its JAX origin.

This time when the lid was pried open and fell to the side, a cloud of fine dust puffed free from the contents, causing the four of us to cough and wave to clear the air in front of our faces. Inside was an official body bag, the black zip-up kind used to transport murder victims from the scenes of crimes and such. Otis reached in and pulled the zipper open. Inside was a curious sight. At a cursory glance I saw that it was a body, all right, but one that looked to have been dead for a long time. Not only that, but it looked to have been embalmed as well, and buried in a formal suit.

"Oh, Christ," Otis gasped. I think this was the first time I'd ever seen him overcome. "April, uh, maybe you should stand over there," he directed me away from the casket.

"Are you kidding?" I was incredulous. "After what I'd been through? I've got actual human gore still speckled on my cargo pants. Believe me, I can handle this." But Otis had whispered something to Officer Ned, and they both turned toward me, shoulder to shoulder, blocking me from further viewing the contents of the casket. LaVonda looked confused and frightened. She held Captain Beefheart to her chest. I tried to push past the two men. "C'mon, let me see," I began to get angry. The two men put their arms around me in an embrace, and refused to let me through. My intuition screamed at me. *Jacksonville,* it said. I smacked the two of them with my fists, tears of anger forming in my eyes. *Jacksonville.*

Here's the thing about intuition; people think it's like a sixth sense or something, like it comes out of nowhere. But it doesn't. Actually, intuition is based on factors that your brain registers but your consciousness hasn't had the time to wrap itself around. To act on your intuition, for example, is to act on this base level of awareness without waiting to validate it consciously. Like once a flight attendant named Anna told me of the time a man asked her for directions. Simple, right? He called out to her from across the street, where he stood holding a map in between two parked cars, a Volkswagen and a van. Anna was on the phone talking to her mother at the time, whom she told to hang on because she was about to walk over and give this here man a hand. That's what flight attendants do, they help people. On the one hand they are trained with an amazing amount of survival skills, but on the other they are also trained to ignore their intuition when it comes to people, lest that intuition interfere with the airline's need for them to behave as handmaiden to the general populace.

Anyway, Anna's mom was a flight attendant as well, but a senior one who had long ago shed the industry's mandate and re-sharpened her intuition. She told Anna, right into her ear, "Don't go near that man. Just keep walking, but first get a good look at him and tell me the license number of the van."

"How do you know there's a van?"

How *did* Anna's mother know there was a van? Intuition, that's how. Anna's mother had been around long enough to have it floating around in the back of her head how predators operate, and one of the ways predators operate is to ask a girl for help. It was kind of genius, really, because who'd be afraid of someone needing help? The van part, well, it was a natural leap. Almost all serial killers had vans on account of how they made excellent combo kidnap/murder workshops on wheels.

A day later a young woman from a few neighborhoods away disappeared. Anna and her mother called the tip line and their subsequent interview with the police helped apprehend the culprit. Unfortunately the girl was found dead. See, she should not have ignored her intuition.

Jacksonville, my intuition screamed at me.

First, why would Otis want to keep me from seeing the contents of the casket? Especially since I'd gotten a glance and seen it wasn't Malcolm in there? Why would Otis be so concerned for my feelings? Especially when he had more confidence in my ability to withstand trauma than I did myself? Why treat me with kid gloves all of a sudden?

I knew the answer. "Really, you two, I can handle it." My voice was calm but my heart jumped around inside my ribs. Officer Ned and Otis looked at each other with uncertainty. "I swear, I'll be all right," I assured them. Silently and reluctantly, the two men stepped aside and allowed me through.

Despite my assurances, as I came closer to the casket, I felt more tears begin to flow. Inside the crate—hands peacefully placed across his chest, funeral makeup now garish against the sunken and dried flesh on his skull, the small rose I had placed under his fingers now aged into a perfect seashell of dried leaves—was my sweet and beloved grandfather Roy Coleman.

Jacksonville was the nearest major airport to St. Augustine, Florida, where until recently he'd been buried next to my grandmother in the peaceful and scenic grounds of Tolomato Cemetery. He died nearly five years ago in his garage while restoring a vintage Ford Rambler. The jack had collapsed, which caused the car to fall on top of him and crush his chest. I remember that when my mother got the news, she cried as hard as she did when my father died. I sat for hours at her feet that day, hugging her legs, while Ash admonished us cruelly. "Get up," he shouted. "Get over it. The guy was old anyway."

A tag on the zipper of my grandfather's body bag matched one clipped to a band on his wrist. They indicated that the remains were to be delivered to the forensic department of the Fulton County coroner's lab.

"That's your grandfather?" LaVonda asked. Otis had updated her as I gazed at the casket. "You poor child. Here, take Beefy Cakes." She handed me the dog and I buried my face in his sweet fur. "What on earth is your poor dead granddaddy doing on this plane?"

I had a feeling it had something to do with the federal subpoena to exhume his remains in order to prove my paternal lineage. I discussed this with the other three, taking care to sound composed since they were all staring at me like I was two seconds from collapsing into a laundry pile saturated with sobs. Officer Ned supported my theory, explaining that the body would have been shipped to Atlanta because the chain of custody required by the subpoena specified the DNA sample to be extracted by the jurisdiction requesting the sample.

"Yeah, that explains why he was in ATL," Otis said, "but why is he here, on this plane? He should have been picked up from the cargo area last night."

Yes, why was he on this plane? To Grand Cayman. The four of us thought deeply for a minute. My intuition started squawking again. *That bastard*, it said. I didn't know why or even how, but I knew Ash Manning had something to do with this.

Otis broke the silence. "Let's close him back up for now." The second he replaced the lid, we heard the aircraft rumble to life around us.

"There's the engines!" Otis, the true machine enthusiast, perked up. "Where're we headed?"

We informed him of the flight plan to Grand Cayman. He rubbed his hands together and grinned. "The Caribbean, nice."

"I see it differently," I said. I'd been there with Flo a few times. She had a friend who worked the beach bar at the Marriott and got us discounted rooms and free cocktails (for Flo, anyway; all I drank was ginger ale). "Who could ask for more in a vacation?" she said. Actually, I could. The island was hardly more than a haven for big conglomerate banks, designer shops, and staggeringly expensive restaurants that catered to pale Western executives on expense accounts. There was no local flavor like you'd find in other Caribbean islands. For example, Jamaica had an amazing culture in comparison.

Even Cancún, a complete armpit taken over by bad frat bars and 20,000 renditions of the exact same T-shirt shop, offered a more colorful atmosphere than Grand Cayman. To me, the island was as fun and welcoming as an expensive toilet. The average Forbes Global 2000 company accountant would probably differ with me, though, since the island had become a magnet for hefty offshore bank accounts ever since Switzerland ceased to be an outlet in that regard. I knew these things from my brief stint on the WorldAir board. It was amazing what files the officials let me look at when they themselves had no idea what they contained.

I felt the portable jet stairs nudge the aircraft. The ramp worker maneuvered them into place at the right-front door above us. We all hushed as we heard the aircraft door open and the footsteps of the pilots, cabin crew, and smattering of company wonks walk onboard.

Officer Ned asked to see the pairing summary again and I handed it to him. "This plane is going to be practically empty," he observed. Yes; I explained to him about how the plane had been purchased by Peacock Airways and the transfer was set to occur at GCM airport. "I'm going up there to talk to the pilots, then." He stepped toward the elevators. Out of habit, I moved to stop him by placing my hand on his arm. I had an inherent distrust of authority while Officer Ned, being an authority figure whose father was an authority figure, had the opposite sentiment. Our views often clashed because of this, which since we've known each other has helped keep us from being too stagnant in our views. Still, I didn't want him to just barge on upstairs without a plan.

He turned to me. "What?" he asked. I was having a hard time voicing my apprehension. "We have to tell the pilots about this."

"Why do we have to tell anyone just yet?" I countered. No one knew we were onboard. It was a perfect situation if you asked me. "Please . . ." I began, but he gently pulled his arm from my grip and turned back toward the elevators.

"April, we have to send someone to check on Flo, for one thing," he reminded me.

Otis straightened with sudden attentiveness. "What about Flo?" he asked. "What happened to Flo?"

LaVonda filled him in on the coded distress signal we received from Flo during our cellphone conversation with her earlier, as well as the *MacGyver* reference. "Season four, episode eleven," she said, nodding solemnly.

At that Otis headed for the elevators himself. "Now where are you going?" I asked. He didn't answer, as just then there was loud clamoring that signaled the elevators were coming to life. LaVonda, now accustomed to concealing herself, rushed to the jumpseat area so she'd be out of the sight line of the elevator window. Otis and I ducked behind the caskets while Officer Ned, worrisomely, stood his ground before the elevator door so that whoever opened it would encounter him before anything else.

At just 16 inches wide, the elevators on an L-1011 are little more than dumbwaiters, really. They can accommodate just one meal cart or two people front-to-back at a time. Either/or, not both. To operate from the inside, two toggle switches on each side of the interior need to be pressed simultaneously, making it impossible to control it with just one hand. This design was intentional, as a legacy of earlier-model, differently designed L-1011s had a propensity for people to get their limbs ripped off. As a mechanic, Uncle Otis was especially knowledgeable about these types of injuries to cabin crew on the aircraft, as he was often dispatched to create adjustments to the machinery to circumvent similar accidents in the future. Otis himself was further testimony that air travel is just a giant ongoing human experiment. Accidents like the Tenerife disaster always result in studies that identify glitches in the system that can be corrected to make flying safer. In that instance, the miscommunication between air traffic control and the KLM pilot centered around the phrase "stand by for takeoff," which was misunderstood as "cleared for takeoff," to horrific consequence. Today, the universal rule during taxi is that the word "takeoff" cannot be spoken in the cockpit during taxi unless it's to inform and confirm that the aircraft is cleared for the runway.

On my mother's refrigerator, she kept a list Otis had made for her benefit, detailing his "top six" most common workplace injuries that occur inside an aircraft cabin. Here's the list:

OTIS'S TOP 6 LIST OF MOST COMMON WORKPLACE INJURIES THAT OCCUR INSIDE AN AIRCRAFT CABIN

1. **Loss of Limb.** In 1976, a stewardess got her hand cut off in the service elevator of an L-1011 when it got stuck between the fuselage and the downward-traveling elevator.
2. **Loss of Eye.** Example: One Uncle Otis Blodgett. 'Nuff said.
3. **Third-Degree Burn.** Until the mid-nineties, when airlines banned inflight smoking, flight attendants commonly ignited like Roman candles thanks to the combination of alcohol, lit cigarettes, and, worst of all, the synthetic fibers that made up their uniforms. ("You might as well wear clothes made out of exploding aerosol cans," Otis said.)

4. **Stab Wound.** And I don't even mean the kind created by knives. An aircraft in the sky is far from a stable environment. Accidental stabbings by Bic pen, umbrella, broken cane, chopsticks, and the like are common.

5. **Head Injury.** Those flying soda cans pack a punch once the plane hits turbulence.

6. **Broken Leg.** Just make sure the beverage cart is secured during takeoff. And if it's not, don't stick your leg in the aisle to stop it from careening toward the passengers. It weighs 700 pounds. (Flo added this one.)

Every time I heard the grinding of the L-1011 elevator gears, I thought of this list. As the elevator descended I could see a set of legs, first. They were clad in the slacks option of the WorldAir flight attendant uniform. This must be one of the cabin crew members, I realized. Even though the flight was being ferried at near-zero passenger capacity, there would still need to be at least two flight attendants to man the front doors. These were the kinds of trips the FAs at WorldAir loved, because they were paid the same for ferry flights as they were for working a plane full of whiney passengers. Ferry flights tended to come available at the last minute, and if you were quick at the employee interface, you could pluck one up for extra time. And if you were lucky you'd get a captain who let you fly the plane, too. Totally against the law, but it happened.

The clamoring stopped once the elevator had fully descended. Officer Ned obstructed my view of inside the car as he stood between me and the elevator. Then, curiously, he held out his arms and let out a hearty laugh. "Oh, my God," he said, his voice thickening with relief, "am I glad to see you."

"Likewise, Thor," Flo said, and walked into his embrace.

CHAPTER 18

"Flo!" I clambered to her side to join in on the hug. She turned toward me and then caught sight of Otis, who had sprung forth from behind the nearest stack of caskets.

"What the *hell*?" she shrieked. "You're dead, you bastard! I heard the ambulance driver say so!" As if to prove to herself that she wasn't hallucinating, she picked up the crowbar from the floor and threw it at him.

Otis turned and winced when it hit him in the butt. "Ouch. Watch it. I've had enough trouble with crowbars lately." Flo wailed with relief and threw herself into his arms.

We explained to her how she wasn't the only one who thought Otis was gone, as we found him in one of the travel caskets just like any other cadaver. "I wasn't dead, I was just rebooting," Otis said, which was as good an explanation as any. LaVonda called for assistance getting free from the jumpseat again, and as I turned to help her I caught sight of someone else in the elevator. He had his back to me—a tall man in an expensive suit—but when he turned around the recognition hit me. I wanted to throw myself through the small door and stick to him like a squid, but I could do little more than just stand there like an idiot, staring at him.

"Hi, April," Malcolm emerged from the elevator and smiled shyly at me.

CHAPTER 19

Finally my motor functions returned and I went to him, blinking back tears of relief. Captain Beefheart flung his pudgy self against his chest, where Malcolm held him close. Beefheart had always been Malcolm's dog, after all. Officer Ned led us into a huddle, where we debriefed each other on the events since yesterday. *Was it really just 24 hours since I saw Malcolm get abducted outside his dad's office?* I marveled.

"Actually, they took me four days ago, not just yesterday. The driver mistook me for my Dad." That driver was Ash Manning, of course, who, as part of the grift, had gotten hired as a driver by Malcolm's mother. (Evidently her background check consisted of one question: "When can you start?") When Hackman realized they got the wrong Colgate, he must have decided to use Malcolm in a ploy to get to his father.

"What did they want with your father?" Officer Ned asked.

"The money he took," Malcolm lowered his head, "—that he stole." They told him his father refused to bend to their demands, even at the risk of Malcolm's own welfare. "Finally they asked me to impersonate him, and I said yes. It's the least I could do."

"What do you mean they *asked* you?" I cried. "It didn't look like they were politely asking you from my perspective. And they *shot* at us."

"Those were just blanks," he shrugged. "They would never hurt any of you. They promised me."

We stared at him, agog. All except Flo, who asked Malcolm to take Beefheart through the bulkhead and down the catwalk in case he had any business to take care of. "And make sure he craps under the pilot hatch so the boys in the cockpit can enjoy the aroma," she laughed.

When Malcolm was out of earshot, she turned to us and lowered her voice. "They got in his head, Crash," she told me. "He thinks he's going to Grand Cayman to get the money and give it back to the people his father stole it from—not just the shareholders, but the pensions of all the employees, and the people who invested their life savings in the stock of Colgate Enterprises. The kidnappers convinced him he's doing the right thing—restoring his family name."

I realized this meant Malcolm thought his father refused to talk even when Hackman threatened his family. Malcolm was under the impression his dad valued the money over him, when the likely truth was the opposite—if his father had given Hackman what he wanted, there would have been no reason for them to keep Malcolm alive. Now here the stupid thugs have killed Mr. Colgate and still didn't have the bank account information. But obviously they thought they no longer needed it, since they'd convinced Malcolm to fly to Grand Cayman and impersonate his father in an attempt to access the funds.

Flo explained that, for her part, she had been able to convince the criminals of her usefulness by suggesting she schedule herself as part of the cabin crew for their flight to Grand Cayman. Malcolm backed her up and that was why she'd been escorted home and back, to change into her uniform.

"And guys," Flo continued, "Malcolm doesn't know his dad's dead."

I gasped and covered my mouth. Poor Malcolm! They must have spent days brainwashing him. "Yeah," Flo said. "They laid it on pretty thick."

Malcolm called to us from the behind the bulkhead to apologize for taking so long. "Beefheart doesn't want to poop."

"That's okay, you take all the time you need," Flo called to him, then turned back to us and lowered her voice.

The two airport ambulance drivers, she explained, were also part of the smuggling scheme. After she hopped in the back of the ambulance with Otis, they brought Flo straight to Hackman's safe house across from the Cheetah strip club, where Malcolm was holed up with Ash and little Miss Chesty GargantoBoobs from the getaway car. It's also the reason the woman didn't kill Flo the second she was dragged through the door by the drivers, because it would have blown her cover as a compassionate do-gooder trying to reunite people with their lost pensions. No matter how brainwashed Malcolm was, I doubt he'd have remained her ally if she killed his friend right in front of him.

"Who *is* that woman?" I asked.

Flo lit a cigarette and eyed me with reluctance. "You're not gonna like this . . ." She shook her head and decided on a different approach. "Okay, they call her Dr. Lullwater. I don't know her first name."

"Dr. Lullwater! She came to my office this morning," Officer Ned exclaimed. "She had *documents.* Here, I kept a copy of her credentials." He reached into his pocket and pulled out a square of printer paper and unfolded it. "This is her badge."

"Right," Flo snorted. "I bet it is."

I peered at the grainy image on the paper. The name on the badge read "Lena Lullwater, Forensic Psychologist, ABPP." The face in the picture, though, read something different altogether. The hair was platinum blonde and the double chin was gone, but I recognized her. I pointed to the image so hard I nearly punched the paper from Officer Ned's hand.

"That's Molly Hackman!"

"I said you weren't gonna like it," said Flo. She was right. I was furious.

"I told you, Thor!" LaVonda piped up. "Did I not TELL you? And here you were ready to hand over our April with a birthday bow." We realized she was still stuck in her seat. Flo reached over and with one twist undid the jumpseat harness so LaVonda could stand, but instead LaVonda remained seated, her hands clasped, listening to us eagerly.

Officer Ned protested. "I wasn't about to hand April over until I heard her side of the story."

"Were too," LaVonda countered, "with a birthday bow."

Exasperated, Officer Ned dropped the back-and-forth. I made sure to let him know it was okay. I forgave him. Molly had really done a number on me as well. It's like she knew exactly how to ingratiate herself into my friendship. Was it also part of her long game to get a job waiting tables at Flo's and my favorite Waffle House in Hapeville? And to think I brought flowers to her hospital room almost every day! Wait . . .

"Who's the woman with her face bashed in at the hospital right now?" I asked Flo.

She took a long drag on her menthol and exhaled the smoke out of the side of her mouth to deflect it from blowing into my face. "No idea, kid."

We heard Malcolm making his way back through the hole in the bulkhead. "You leave that poor child to me," LaVonda whispered to us, her trauma training kicking in. "Don't nobody tell him a thing about his dad. We have to handle this one tiny piece at a time."

Before Malcolm rejoined us, Flo turned to Officer Ned to address another dire subject. "Looks like you have a huge problem to deal with, Thor," she intoned, explaining that a gang of airport security officers and ambulance drivers had been in cahoots with Hackman on a smuggling ring.

"Drugs? Do NOT tell me they are smuggling drugs!" gasped LaVonda.

"Not drugs," Flo said. "Counterfeit airplane parts."

Otis stiffened with attention. Airplane parts were his territory. They were violating his territory! *"Which parts?"*

Flo took another drag and shook her head. Me? I wasn't surprised. Criminals, not to mention those who are just desperate to escape their circumstances, were figuring out new ways every day to smuggle contraband across country borders—human, animal, and otherwise. I'd befriended a veteran customs agent at the Atlanta airport who worked the afternoon shift that met most of the flights arriving from South America. He was a wealth of information. He told me about the time a lady tried to smuggle a sedated baby white tiger in a suitcase with a bunch of stuffed tiger toys, and the time a woman tried to smuggle her husband's dead body out of the country by buying it a ticket and trying to push it on the plane in a wheelchair. When she was caught she said she thought he was just sleeping. But the counterfeit airplane parts, that was especially odious.

"How are they smuggling the parts?" Officer Ned interrupted.

Suddenly it came to me with the clarity of a cowbell. "I know how they're smuggling the parts," I said. "They're stuffing them inside the dead bodies." And when the corpses were slow in coming, they created their own by killing a few coworkers in their vicinity. That would explain the missing airport employees.

"Think about it," I continued. "They must have been deflecting the casket cargo to Grand Cayman, where they probably have some setup that allows them to stash the contraband inside the corpses before they're shipped back."

"But why Grand Cayman?" Officer Ned asked. Flo and I shrugged. The island was part of the British Antilles and probably stuffed to busting with corrupt, greasy-palmed officials who had no qualms about threading unidentified dead bodies through their coroner's lab and back again.

"And what are the plane parts that are being falsified?" Otis was insistent and I understood why. Counterfeit engine parts don't undergo any quality control at all, let alone the rigorous strength testing that clears any standard part for use in an aircraft. That's why these parts were so expensive—some costing upwards of hundreds of thousands of dollars apiece—because they had been forged with meticulous precision and tested to guarantee durability. This was also why the counterfeit market was so lucrative, because counterfeit parts could be made for pennies and sold to unsuspecting airlines for the same markup as real ones. Right now, millions of lives were at risk if unsound parts were being used to repair and update aircraft engines. "Which parts?" Otis repeated.

"Wait," I reached into my cargo pocket and retrieved the sandwich bag containing the curious octagonal-shaped objects I'd collected yesterday. "This came from one of the corpses last night . . ."

"Ew." LaVonda covered her face with the crook of her arm, but hours ago I'd used the galley sink to clean the gunk off the pieces as best I could, so they weren't that bad. Otis took one from me and examined it closely with his good eye.

"See there?" I indicated some tiny raised numerals on the underside.

"Yes. 'V-2927-PRES45.'" He slipped the counterfeit part into his pocket. "This is not good." Part number V-2927-PRES45, he explained, was a sophisticated new circuit breaker for the aircraft's pressurization panel. The FTSB had recently mandated that all WorldAir jets were to be retrofitted with this device by the end of November, as well as the jets of all other airlines based in the United States and those outside the U.S. with routes into and out of our country. These kinds of mandates were constantly levied by the federal Department of Transportation in response to new information regarding aviation accidents.

Because, like I said, air travel was an ongoing human experiment. Every time a plane crashed, the practice would be to figure out what failure—mechanical or human—caused it, then retrofit all remaining aircraft to safeguard against it happening again. Take Tuninter flight 1153, which, after both engines failed, crashed into the Mediterranean Sea, killing half the people onboard. When the investigators salvaged the engines from the ocean, they could find nothing wrong with them, concluding that the aircraft simply ran out of fuel because the wrong kind of fuel gauge had been installed in the cockpit. It was that simple—a matter of kilograms versus gallons. Since that accident, the FTSB had implemented a mass gauge replacement so a mistake like this can never occur again. For this reason, the manufacturing of new aircraft replacement parts is an immensely profitable business.

But sometimes the cause of a plane wreck was a mystery that never got solved. A devastating case in point would be WorldAir flight 0392, which disappeared without a trace over the Pacific Ocean between Hawaii and Sydney, Australia, last November. *Not a trace* of the 747 or the hundreds of passengers and crew contained therein have been found. Conspiracy theories abounded, many of them from Otis, who kept an ongoing list. Here it is:

OTIS'S ONGOING LIST OF CONSPIRACY THEORIES INVOLVING THE FATE OF WORLDAIR FLIGHT 0392

1. **Life Insurance Scam.** One or more of the people onboard had a hefty death policy, the beneficiaries of which somehow engineered the destruction of the jet midflight.
2. **Hijacking.** The plane was flown to a remote area in Afghanistan, where the passengers are alive and living in mud huts, subsisting on insects and rainwater.
3. **Abducted by Aliens.** YouTube footage shows the presence of extraterrestrials over the seventh archipelago. (Could be doctored footage.)
4. **Accidentally Shot Down in Army Training Exercise.** A New Zealand oil-rig worker claims to have seen the plane go down in flames into the Gulf of Thailand, where multinational army training maneuvers were under way.

5. **Deliberately Shot Down**, prompting an international cover-up.

6. **Hijacking Theory #2.** The plane was forcibly redirected and flown in the shadow of another passenger jet traveling to Siberia. Passengers are alive and living in ice huts, subsisting on sardines and melted snow.

I've spent an inordinate amount of time agonizing over the mystery myself. It was a particular sore spot with me, because I'd known two of the flight attendants onboard the plane.

The intercom crackled to life. "We're third in line. Prepare the cabin for takeoff," the pilot instructed. We had about ten minutes before we were in the air. LaVonda hooted fearfully and did a scaled-down version of her back-and-forth panic dance. Then, out of habit, she sat in the jumpseat and buckled up. Malcolm, who had made it back from behind the bulkhead with Beefheart, eyed her with amused curiosity.

"We need to get upstairs," Flo moved toward the elevators, then stopped and turned back to us. "I mean all of us. You can't stay down here during takeoff. It's dangerous."

She was right; the jumpseats located in the lower galley were there for inflight only, not for takeoff. We'd have to go upstairs and take passenger seats. Flo sensed my nervousness. "There's only a few people up there," she said. "They'll never know you're onboard." She dowsed her cigarette in the galley sink, adding, "Probably."

I shrugged. An L-1011 was the length of two city blocks. Things commonly occurred at one end of the plane that remained completely unknown to the people at the other. Especially when the engines were running, because the engines drowned out all other sounds. Recently while a flight to Dallas sat on the runway waiting for takeoff, a passenger near the last row mistook the air-conditioning condensation as smoke coming from the vents and tried to incite a panicked spontaneous evacuation of the aircraft. It took ten minutes for the flight attendants in back to get the passengers to stop screaming, while those in first class, with their earphones, cocktails, and complete lack of situational awareness, had no idea anything unusual was happening behind them.

We lined up to ride up to the passenger cabin. Flo and Malcom first, next me and Officer Ned, then Otis and LaVonda. It was a lumbering process and I debated just climbing up through the escape hatch that opened into the passenger aisle above, but decided that might draw attention. As a general rule I considered attention to be bad, believe me. I missed the days up until last year when I could sail through airport security and customs wearing a tiara made out of pipe bombs if I wanted. But those days ended when I became a public piñata in the news. Now it felt like I could barely walk to the drugstore without a SWAT team swarming down.

As Flo stepped into the elevator with Malcolm I heard LaVonda ask, "Wait, that was Morse code, right? On the phone earlier?"

Flo looked at her like she was nuts. "Are you nuts? I was making a batch of Bloody Marys." As if to emphasize her point, she produced a flask from her apron pocket and took a swig.

Officer Ned said, "But the *MacGyver* reference, that was to let us know your phone was tapped, right?"

Flo shook her head and took another swig. "Amateurs," she said. "Tell 'em, Crash."

I had no idea. Flo closed the elevator door before I could get her to clarify. The *MacGyver* episode in question differed from most in that it didn't deal with overt espionage, but a family-law situation in which a boy had been kidnapped by his noncustodial father. Turned out the father was the nephew of a crime boss and, you know, hijinks ensued.

Flo sent the elevator back down for Officer Ned and me, but he was too big and tall to fit in with me, so I entered it alone, flipped the toggle switches, and began my ascent. It was actually one of my favorites, that *MacGyver* episode. The father was a narcissistic wonk who only wanted the child for selfish reasons. Given my history with Ash, I could totally relate. When I was a kid he used to insist my mother bid for long overnight trips just so he could leave me locked in the house while he partied with his friends. I remember the neighbors once sent the police over after hearing me cry all night, only to have Ash return in time to intercept them at the door and convince them that the college sophomore in the car with him was actually my babysitter and there was nothing to worry about. In the *MacGyver* episode Flo mentioned, the crime boss character provided an interesting twist, because he ended up having a change of heart and siding with the mother.

This was on my mind as I exited the lift and stepped into the midgalley of the L-1011. I opened the door to see Anita standing there in a flight attendant uniform. *Anita! Why is Anita here?* I was actually happy to see her, but before I could cry out in surprise, she crossed the galley in two quick steps and angrily punched me in the face.

CHAPTER 20

"Ouch! What the . . ." I grabbed my jaw, stumbled backward, and felt for a jumpseat to sit down. I sat in a passenger seat instead. The jet accelerated down the runway. Free of the weight of passengers, it lifted into the air almost immediately. The floor pitched. Anita stumbled after me and raised her hand to hit me again. I looked up in shock. It did not even occur to me to strike back.

"That's enough, Teddy," Molly Hackman told her. *Teddy?* "I don't want her dead just yet. Take her to the midcabin with the others." In her hand Molly cupped the gun I'd used to shoot her husband, the one I gave Flo before I went into hiding.

Most people have the assumption that a firearm can't be dispatched in an airplane cabin without causing an explosive decompression. But that assumption is an exaggeration. Most of the time the bullet would just lodge itself in something in the interior of the plane—a seat, meal cart, bulkhead, *body*. If this happened, of course, the cabin air would not be compromised because there'd be no damage to the skin of the fuselage. Now if the bullet actually pierced the aluminum skin, there would of course be cause for alarm, but no reason for panic, per se, because modern jets are built to withstand this level of damage. The hole would create a small leak, but the pressurization system was designed to compensate for it. Even a few holes like this would have no effect on the integrity of the aircraft.

But if the bullet blew out part of the structure, that would be a problem. Damage like that could cause a domino effect leading, in seconds, to a catastrophic depressurization. Consider that Aloha Airlines flight that turned into a midair convertible in 1988 because of "metal fatigue"—a crevice in the plane's aluminum skin corroded over time until it created enough friction to rip the roof off the plane midflight. Astoundingly only one person died in that accident—a flight attendant, of course. If only she'd been strapped in, she would not have been caught up in the debris that got sucked out of the opening.

The plane leveled and Anita yanked me to my feet. "I'm sorry, I'm sorry, I'm sorry!" she whispered to me as she made a big show of shoving me around. "Just act scared, okay? And I'm sorry!" I was so relieved this was an act—that she hadn't turned bad after all—that I immediately forgave her despite the stinging in my jaw.

"What's with the 'Teddy' business?" I asked. She hushed me and shoved me into a seat next to Flo. Officer Ned, who had come up in the elevator after me, was directed by Molly's gun to take the seat across the aisle from us. Molly handed Anita the zip-tie handcuffs from the cockpit flight kit and instructed her to bind our wrists. All cockpit flight kits contained four sets of these handcuffs for the purpose of neutralizing unruly passengers should the occasion arise. Unlike normal zip-ties, which are easy to pop free from, if you ask me, these plastic cuffs were super thick and made specifically to subdue people. In her zeal to appear authentically henchman-like, Anita pulled the zip-ties really tight around our wrists. There was one left over, which Molly told her to use to bind Officer Ned's ankles together.

Malcolm sat up front in the first row behind the cockpit. Otis and LaVonda had not come up from the galley. In fact, LaVonda may well have been stuck in the jumpseat below again. I noticed the badge clipped to Anita's pocket flap. "Teddy LaVista," it read. I turned to Flo.

"That's the badge Otis gave you in the parking lot!" I whispered.

"I told you, they never look."

I'll say, the only thing Anita had in common with the man in the badge was that she was also African American. Flo explained to me that she figured out the real Teddy LaVista was part of Hackman's smuggling ring, a person Molly only knew as a name on a list Hackman had made and magnetized to their refrigerator. When Molly escorted Flo back to her house to collect her uniform, they'd found Anita there sitting on the stoop, holding Trixi. The only way Flo could keep Molly from turning Anita into another dead smuggling mule was to slip Anita the badge and introduce her as "my roommate, Teddy LaVista, who lost her key again."

It probably helped that the name "Teddy" could be loosely construed as a girl's name, and, again, Anita was holding Trixi at the time. Molly, it turned out, had known that Mr. Colgate fed the button containing the microprocessor to her dog—

that much Hackman had been able to get out of him before torturing him to death—and was so elated to be reunited with Trixi that she credited Anita with the pup's return. Before long, Anita was getting outfitted into a spare uniform and listening to hushed instructions from Flo to act tough.

"What does this have to do with the clue you dropped about the *MacGyver* episode?" Officer Ned whispered, exasperated.

Flo lit a cigarette, barely encumbered by her bound wrists. "You two never understand my *MacGyver* references. I'm way over your heads."

Molly stood nearby, assuring we saw the gun in her hand. She carried a large Nike rucksack on her back. She approached us and snapped the cigarette from Flo's fingers. Rather than snuff it out on the carpet like I expected her to do, she started smoking it herself. Flo grumbled and unwrapped a stick of gum.

"You can't point the gun at all of us," Officer Ned challenged her.

"You're right," she agreed, "but one of you will do." She aimed the gun at my head.

"Molly . . ." I began.

"Not a word from you." She took another drag from the cigarette, furious. "It's like a cloud of chaos follows you wherever you go. You would not believe the cleanup I've had to perform since yesterday."

I held my tongue. The most pressing question in my mind, I'm ashamed to say, had to do with her newly minted double-D cups, not to mention the fresh platinum Betty Boop hairdo. Today she looked less like a Waffle House waitress and more like a Las Vegas cocktail waitress. Molly saw where I was staring and read my mind. "Costa Rican plastic surgery."

She smiled. "Part of the perks of being married to a crooked airline mechanic—free travel and all the implants you want."

"Not to mention liposuction," mumbled Flo. Molly shot her a look that shut her up.

"Do you see that boy up there?" she pointed toward Malcolm in the front cabin. "He'll do anything I ask. He's devoted to me. And why wouldn't he be?" Her face turned sarcastic. "The poor kid—a father who didn't love him enough to confess where he kept the money he stole, a mother who ran off and can't be bothered to answer the phone."

Here she was really hitting a nerve with me. Malcolm and I had been best friends since our days as unaccompanied minors, crisscrossing the coasts to accommodate the custody schedules of parents who seemed more concerned with sticking it to each other than the welfare of their kids. We had been through so much together, Malcolm and I, that I considered him an essential part of my life. Lately, as this business about his father's fraudulent actions hit the fan—the indictment, the media, the *shame*—Malcolm had begun to spend more and more time with me and Flo. We were careful to never mention the indictment and strived to create a safe emotional haven for him, but still he seemed to retreat emotionally, sometimes to the point where he would simply sit with us, staring blankly for hours. I could always bring him around, though. Sometimes it took awhile, but eventually I could bring him back. Now here this horrible woman had taken advantage of Malcolm's fragile state and gotten her hooks in him. I fumed visibly. If anything happened to Malcolm . . . I just . . . I don't know what I'd do. I had a hard time breathing just thinking about it. I mean, *his own mother* couldn't be bothered to . . .

Suddenly it occurred to me where Malcolm's mother was.

"That's Mrs. Colgate in the hospital, isn't it?" I seethed, but I already knew the answer. Same size and general physique of the former Molly, and a face beaten into an unrecognizable pulp. How convenient that all you had to do to name a comatose assault victim was to have the next of kin identify the person. In this case Hackman probably simply told the ER personnel that the woman was his wife. Bing bang boom. Instant life-insurance settlement, but for one small snag.

"Damn you." Molly glared at me. I see why she was mad; if I hadn't kept Hackman from pulling the plug at the hospital, they'd be half a million richer right now. Instead, my friend Alby was now the legal guardian of Molly, or actually the unfortunate Mrs. Colgate, whom Hackman had chosen to be Molly's stunt double.

The flight deck opened and Ash made it halfway down the aisle before he saw me and Officer Ned, then he did a swift 180 back to the cockpit, where he furtively knocked on the door, asking to be let back in.

"Just one question," I implored Molly. She shrugged and took another hit off of the cigarette she'd appropriated from Flo.

"Why the Waffle House?" I asked. "I mean, of all places."

"I was wondering that, too," Flo said.

Molly exhaled. "Malcolm's dad was a big fan. We had him staked out as a mark for months, and we noticed that he stopped in there on his way in and out of town, like clockwork. Turns out he had a thing for Waffle House waitresses." Flo and I snorted. Molly glowered at us. "What's so funny? It happens."

On second thought it made sense. There were countless websites devoted to stewardess fetishes, why not waitresses? Both professions trained them to be subservient, right? And then over time some wire snaps in their head and they become "sassy" instead. I theorized this was why Flo collected ex-husbands like postage stamps. She seemed to have the same Jedi mind-trick effect over gentlemen that Otis had over women. Play it right and it's like a super power. I bet a Waffle House waitress fetish wasn't that uncommon.

"He was crazy about me," Molly jutted out her chin proudly. "Bought me a Vegas wedding and a house and everything." So the mansion in Alpharetta was not bought with Hackman's bribe money after all, but as a love token from Mr. Colgate. I wonder how many rich old dudes Hackman and Molly had teamed up on before this one. Mr. Colgate probably pillow-talked about the Cayman accounts, and Hackman and Molly no doubt thought they hit the mother lode. I turned my head toward the window in disgust. *Wait, were we descending already?*

"Where did you get the badge?" Officer Ned intoned gravely. It was obviously a sore spot with him, since he'd belly-upped like a puppy when she showed up at his office this morning claiming to be an FBI forensic psychologist. "It's a federal offense to impersonate an agent of the FBI, you know," he continued.

Now it was Molly's turn to snort. "The badge belonged to one of the bodies we hoodwinked last month. It was in her casket along with her personal things. She died while vacationing alone—fell off the top of a pyramid in Peru." She examined her nails. "Probably a suicide. Anyway, I figured it couldn't hurt to keep the badge. You'd be surprised how easy it is to swap out the pictures on these things."

"The FBI would never be fooled by that."

"I wasn't trying to fool the FBI." She laughed hoarsely at Officer Ned. "Just you. And it worked pretty good."

"You're in big trouble, young lady."

"Oh my *gawd*, seriously?" She laughed again. She was way worse than her husband, I realized. A sociopath with real skill at homing in on the weaknesses of her marks, then transforming herself to fill the voids. "Do you think for a second," she continued, "that I'd be telling you any of this—any of you—if I planned to let you live?"

"Wait," I backtracked. "Malcolm, he would never, *ever*, agree to this. *Malcolm*!" I called up the aisle to him.

Molly seemed unperturbed by my statements. Flo began looking around nervously. Where were Otis and LaVonda? "Who you looking for, sweetie?" Molly asked us with saccharine sweetness. "Worried about your friends?"

We didn't answer. A sinking feeling grew in my gut. "Huh?" she goaded me. "Worried are ya?" I stood, ready to run to the galley, anywhere, to try to find them. *"Sit back down,"* Molly hissed ferociously. I did as she said, nervously glancing at Flo and Officer Ned, who seemed as edgy as me. "I had our friend Ash decompress the cargo area, which as you know includes the galley."

Flo and I looked at each other in alarm. Cabin pressurization is necessary in an aircraft traveling above 10,000 feet, because the air at higher altitudes contains too little oxygen per cubic foot for human sustenance. Thus the airplane "cabin pressure," which creates an atmosphere that is comfortable for passengers. The cabin pressure is usually adjusted automatically, with air from the engines operating at the compressor stage. The air is then treated in all kinds of ways—cooled, humidified, mixed with recirculated air if necessary—and dispersed throughout the cabin by environmental control systems. All this so the passengers could, like, *survive*. This was why the trend of people trying to stow away in the wheel wells of jumbo jets was so deadly—at that altitude, and outside the aircraft cabin, they suffocated in seconds.

Molly's face was smug. She looked at her watch, "I give them about . . ."

She didn't finish, because Officer Ned, with a furious roar, launched himself at her. He caught her at her midsection and they both fell into the aisle. Molly's backpack broke her fall and she was able to kick herself away from him, but he lunged at her again. I knew Officer Ned wasn't thinking rationally, as he was severely restricted by his bound wrists and legs. But Molly had hit a nerve when she threatened LaVonda. As much as he complained about LaVonda, I knew Officer Ned loved her like a little sister. Hell, everyone loved LaVonda. Flo and I stood up and ran to the back galley. I had already picked one of my wrists free from the zip-tie handcuffs, which have a toggle-and-tongue mechanism similar to that of the metal variety, and within seconds freed one of Flo's wrists as well. With our remainder cuffs dangling, we set about our actions.

Here's the thing: All WorldAir jet-cabin jumpseats are stocked with emergency equipment such as flashlights, fire extinguishers, first-aid kits, etc.—and PBUs (portable breathing units). These PBUs are like big inflatable space helmets, to be used in the event of a fire onboard the aircraft. It's made of yellow flame-resistant plastic and silver flame-retardant insulation. The device enables the flight attendant to traverse a smoke-filled cabin to address the source of the fire without succumbing to smoke inhalation. Essentially, the flight attendant activated the helmet by popping apart two CO_2 cylinders at the neck opening and slipping it over her head. The helmet then inflated with air. The time of useful oxygen was just seven minutes.

Flo grabbed the PBU from its slot against the bulkhead, broke apart the cylinders, and slipped the helmet over her head. Immediately it inflated around her face. Her lips were set in a grim line as she entered the elevator and nodded to me through the yellow fire-resistant face mask. She looked so much like a sci-fi character that I would have laughed if the situation weren't so serious. I tossed her another PBU unit I'd found in the overhead bin above the galley jumpseat, and saw her close the door and begin her descent.

Each jumpseat also has a nearby portable-oxygen bottle (referred to as PO2s in the industry) for those common inflight cases when a passenger passes out or just plain hyperventilates from all the suppressed fear and stress that is the inescapable bane of air travel. (Seriously, very common.) I ran to the place where the PO2 unit should have been, only to find an empty bracket. *Damn*! Usually this flight would not have been cleared to take off without all the emergency equipment in place, but since this was a ferried flight with no revenue passengers, the plane didn't have to meet the safety standards of the NTSB.

I ran to the back of the plane to the other set of jumpseats to see if the correct equipment was stowed back there. Luckily it was. I grabbed the PO2 bottle and sped back toward the mid. The PO2 bottle was cumbersome, as it was a big metal cylinder and weighed almost 13 pounds. A glance out the window had me wondering again; *are we descending?* If we were, it was gradual enough not to be too alarming. Pilots get instructed to rise and fall to different altitudes all the time to avoid upcoming turbulence and the like.

Malcolm had made his way to the mid with Anita behind him, until he was standing above Officer Ned and Molly, now a writhing pile of limbs each trying to get power over the other. Bound as he was, Officer Ned could do little more than use his body as a kind of human club to try to physically contain her. Finally Molly wrestled free to stand above him. Officer Ned still struggled in the aisle, trying to get upright. She pointed the gun at his head and pulled the trigger.

CHAPTER 21

I know I mentioned before that Officer Ned was fast. In fact, he was a former linebacker for a professional football team (the name of which he's asked me to never mention) (okay, it starts with "D" and ends with "etroit Lions"), so all I could conclude is that between the time Molly pulled the trigger and the bullet hit him, Officer Ned had positioned his body so that the bullet, rather than entering his skull, sank into his upper arm.

Officer Ned hollered in pain, and the sound soaked into me like acid. Molly smirked with satisfaction and raised the gun to take aim again. This time Officer Ned made an easier target, as he'd passed out from shock. She placed the barrel against his forehead and squeezed the trigger.

I can't explain what happened next except to simply recount it as it transpired. First, there is such a thing as "hysterical strength" in humans. You hear about it all the time, like when the 90-pound granny lifted the truck off her grandson, or the young Canadian woman physically fought off a polar bear—hand-to-paw—to save the two children it was attacking. This strength is caused by adrenaline, evidently, and is beyond what is believed to be humanly normal.

Now, I mentioned earlier that I am skinny, with arms like broomsticks. So I can't explain how I did this except to say that on my physical, *conscious* level I saw Molly put that gun to Officer Ned's head, I saw her pull the trigger—I saw it—but on my reflexes level I must have acted faster than my own eyes. Because before I could register what I'd done, I had hurled that big-ass oxygen bottle through the air and down the aisle like it was a pebble I'd picked up on the side of a creek. I remember watching it spin through the distance like a fat green helicopter blade, wondering, consciously, "Where the hell did that come from?" while I reflexively continued to move forward.

The PO2 bottle hit Molly square in the chest and she fell backward. Her firearm discharged into the ceiling before scuttling from her grip to land somewhere under the center seats. The oxygen masks dropped and a high-pitched ringing sound filled the air as the cabin adjusted to the change in pressure from the hole in the fuselage. I grabbed an inflight blanket and ran to Officer Ned's side to put pressure against his wound. "Malcolm, help me!" I called. He stood frozen in place.

"Malcolm, help me!" Molly called. She put out her hand and Malcolm took it to assist her to her feet. She turned to me, her back to him, brushed herself off, and addressed me with haughty assuredness.

"See?" she said. "He'll do anything I say." She noticed my gaze and turned around to see Malcolm pointing the gun she'd just dropped. "Shoot her!" she demanded. "Do it!" Malcolm raised the gun. I shook my head, my eyes pleading. "That's a good boy," Molly grinned. But then Malcolm pointed the gun at Molly instead. "No," he said, suddenly shaking with fury. "*No!*"

Molly was swift, already on him. She snatched the gun back away from him and he grabbed her wrist. Another bullet discharged into a passenger seat. Then another into the window at the end of the aisle next to them. Finally Molly got the gun free from their struggle and pointed it at Malcolm.

"I don't need you!" she shouted. "I've got the dog, which means I have the microprocessor with the account numbers. I don't need you!" She pulled the trigger. *Click.* She tried again. *Click.*

Click. Click, Click. Click.

"Give it up!" I yelled. "It's out of bullets!" But then I realized the sound wasn't coming from her gun.

Click. Click, Click. Click.

Malcolm and I knew what was happening before Molly did. He turned to tackle Anita into the row of center seats, scrambling to secure their seatbelts. I ran forward and reached for Molly just as the window gave way, leaving a jagged gaping hole in the side of the fuselage.

Here's the thing: During flight, an aircraft cabin is a sealed system that is *under pressure.* Whenever a pressurized, sealed system is breached unexpectedly—such as in this case, when the bullet hole caused enough structure fatigue to blow out the window—it creates that "rapid decompression" I talked about earlier. It causes the opening to act like a black hole of sorts, sucking through it everything nearby that is not tied down—sucking it out and into the wild blue yonder.

Unfortunately for Molly and me, we were not tied down. Even more unfortunately for her, she was closer to the window and had turned toward the noise. She hardly had time to scream before she flew, as if drawn by a monstrous vacuum, toward the jagged opening. There she became wedged, front-first, with a sickening splat against the fuselage, plugging the gap like a big bag of meat.

"Molly!" I cried, and ran to her. My hands found the straps of her backpack. I grabbed them and pulled with all my might. Small rivulets of blood appeared at the seams of the hole and spread out like thin spider legs. She must have suffered some deep lacerations against the jagged edges of the metal. Anita screamed and Malcolm put his arms around her, turning her away. He turned back to me.

"I'm coming to you!" he yelled.

"No!" I implored. "Stay back!"

He hollered something in response, but I barely heard him against the deafening roar of the failing aircraft, which screamed under the pressure of the compromised fuselage. I braced my foot against the armrest of the seat and held on tight, but Molly wouldn't budge. At least not in my direction. Instead it felt as if the center of her was, like, *sinking* into the hole.

How is this happening? I thought, and then it came to me with horrifying clarity. Her skin had been lacerated. The power of the wind against an aircraft traveling at 385 miles per hour was monstrous. If a small fissure can cause enough friction to rip the roof off of a 737, imagine the damage the wind can cause to a gash in a human torso.

Oh, my God! I realized. *She's being degloved!*

I don't know why I held on, even through the revolting rattle I felt as her insides emptied out of her. But I couldn't let go. Molly's skin was no match against the gravitational force of the sucking wind. Eventually her body began to crush in on itself, like a dying star. Her arms and legs bent backward unnaturally, like limp tentacles, then she slipped out of the rucksack and was gone.

I was so stunned I didn't feel myself getting pulled toward the opening myself until I was against it. I could hear Malcolm's screams as I struggled to gain purchase, but with nothing to pull against I'd lost my leverage. Cocktail napkins, blankets, oxygen masks ripped from the ceiling flew by me and out the window. I watched them flutter into oblivion. The plane, engineered to descend automatically in the event of a sudden decompression, tilted sideways in order to drop as quickly as possible. Unfortunately I was on the bottom of the vertical tilt. The autopiloted maneuver made it worse for me. Horrifically, I felt myself pass through the opening.

The funniest things go through your head when you're about to die. Like in this instance. My long hair was already through the opening and slapping against the exterior of the airplane. You'd expect I'd be thinking about my mother, and how her heart would snap in half like a redwood at the news of my demise, or my maternal grandparents, who were with her on the cruise in the Antarctic right now, and how their vacation would be ruined when the purser knocked on their cabin door to present them a terrible telegram, or even the terror at the horrible fate that awaited me after I fell thousands of feet into the rough ocean below. But no, I thought none of those things. As I was about to fly out of the airplane, I felt my pant leg catch on something, and I thought, *Christ, please don't let me get sucked out without my pants. I am NOT going to be found floating ass-naked in the ocean. My half-nude body is NOT gonna wash up on the shore of Cancún in front of a bunch of drunk frat boys. No . . .*

". . . you are NOT!"

Wait, was that LaVonda's voice?

"Honey child, you are NOT fallin' off this plane."

Then I realized it wasn't my pant leg that was caught, but my ankle, and it was caught in someone's grip. "No you are NOT!" LaVonda shouted again. She sounded like she was hollering from a far-off mountaintop. I looked back to see she was wearing the portable breathing unit Flo had taken her. Her face was resolute through the thick yellow plastic that made up the face mask of the inflated helmet.

Look at LaVonda, so serious. I giggled.

The lack of oxygen had caused me to feel an odd elation. Then giddiness overtook my starved brain, and I became certain that if I flew out of the plane right then I'd land safely on the backs of dolphins or something.

I'll be fine, I thought, languidly smacking at LaVonda's grip on my ankle. *Seriously, I'll be fine.*

LaVonda grabbed an oxygen mask from the row ahead of me, one that hadn't been ripped from its ballast by the wind force, and secured it to my face. The cabin pressure was now near equalized, as the aircraft had dropped to within 12,000 feet of the earth's surface, so the suction from the breach in the fuselage had mercifully ceased, though the oxygen density was still very thin.

"Breathe, sweetie," LaVonda hollered through her helmet, which had begun to deflate. She pulled it from her head and grabbed another mask for herself. Within seconds my oxygen-starved brain regained rationality, and the terror of our situation returned. I threw my arms around LaVonda and we struggled over the seatbacks in front of us until we found a row with functioning safety belts. We strapped ourselves in. Suddenly, with a massive centrifugal force, the plane righted itself from its lateral dive. The plane was back in parallel position above the earth, or, in this case, the ocean. But for how long? The engines were wailing from the strain of the ailing aircraft.

"Officer Ned!" I shouted, panicked. I struggled to undo my seatbelt. I had to get to him, assess his bullet wound. LaVonda put one hand over mine assuredly, then gestured with the other to draw my attention behind us. Officer Ned was in the aisle seat a few rows behind Malcolm and Anita. He was pale and bleeding, but his eyes were open above the mask around his nose and mouth. Wide open. His lungs heaved in panicked breaths. Clutched to his chest with both bound hands was Captain Beefheart. Officer Ned must have caught the dog as it flew toward the hole along with the loose cabin debris. Panic caught me again.

"Where's the other dog, Trixi?" I cried.

LaVonda's eyes were wide and sad as she shrugged her shoulders.

Soon the cabin pressure was fully equalized, making the oxygen masks unnecessary. I tore mine off, undid my seatbelt, and stood. The others remained still, staring at me. The hole in the fuselage still gaped, the sound of the roaring wind was deafening, but with the cabin pressure equalized, we no longer needed to worry about falling off the plane unless we stepped through it. The first to follow my suit was Malcolm. He undid his seatbelt, helped Anita to her feet, and directed her to the forward cabin, as far away from the blown window as possible. I tried to do the same with LaVonda, but she resisted me. Instead we headed back to Officer Ned.

Officer Ned handed Captain Beefheart to LaVonda and she took the seat across the aisle from him. We were still too close to the gaping hole in the fuselage for me to be at all comfortable, but LaVonda was right. Officer Ned needed to be freed from his restraints before we could do anything further. I took out my picks and, with shaking fingers, took about twice as long to release the cuffs as I should have, but still the process was deft.

I indicated for him to remove his belt, then I used it to secure the passenger pillow against his bullet wound in order to stave off the bleeding. Thankfully the bullet did not seem to have hit a major artery. Still, Officer Ned looked weak and ashen.

He stood shakily, and just as I hooked myself under his arm to assist him to the front cabin, the plane seemed to hit an air pocket, causing us to drop an additional hundred feet. Officer Ned and I found ourselves first flat against the ceiling and then jackhammered over the seatbacks before the plane righted itself. LaVonda screamed. She turned sideways in her seat, hooked her legs around Officer Ned's torso, and, with her spare hand still grasping Captain Beefheart, she hooked her other hand into the waistband of my cargo pants. It was a good thing, too, because almost as quickly as we fell, we rose again. I knew air pockets seldom came in single incidents, but we weren't just falling—we were oscillating. Our plane was nearly nose-up parallel to the earth's surface, when suddenly we crested and dove nose down again. We repeated the roller-coaster ride a few more times before the plane appeared to stabilize.

What the hell is going on in the cockpit? I thought. This effect was called "porpoising," after how a porpoise dives up and down, in and out of the water—or the more technical term, "pilot-induced oscillation." Miraculously, the three of us (four, if you count Captain Beefheart) were kept from being tossed around like rag dolls thanks to LaVonda and her single seatbelt.

Once LaVonda was sure the plane was finished with its yo-yo tricks, she let go and we resumed our progress to the front cabin. LaVonda handed Beefheart to Malcolm, who cried out gratefully. Anita sat next to them in the row directly behind the front bulkhead, closest to the door. Their faces were white with fear, but still they rose to help us with Officer Ned. We strapped him in a center seat, where I changed the bandage I'd fashioned for him earlier with a fresh pillow. I opened the overhead bin to get the emergency medical kit all commercial aircraft are supposed to have onboard, only to find one that had been half depleted from a prior use. Was there nothing on this plane compliant with the safety standards of the Federal Aviation Administration? Even the bustle containing the emergency escape raft was missing from the left-front door.

Damn it, I worried. Where's Flo? Her pockets were probably packing a few painkillers that Officer Ned could use right now. I looked around the small galley for anything I could use. I opened the liquor kit to grab some bottles of alcohol as an impromptu disinfectant. I blindly grabbed at the minis, shoved them into my cargo pockets, and continued rummaging. Just then the cockpit door opened, flooding the cabin with sunlight from the front windshield. I expected Ash to be standing there, or perhaps the captain—neither of whom had been seen or heard from since the breach in the fuselage—but no.

"Hey, kid, we're out of vodka. Believe me, I looked."

"Flo!" I yelled. I would have hugged her but there wasn't time. She stepped aside so I could enter the cockpit. Otis was in the copilot's seat, doing his best to control the aircraft. *Why isn't he in the captain's seat?* I wondered. *And what's that noise?* Then it occurred to me. On the captain's side of the flight deck, the windshield was missing. That noise was the wind roaring through the opening—that and Uncle Otis, who was hooting and howling like a crazed wolf.

Where's Ash? I thought. *Where's the copilot?*

"I don't know," Flo answered me. I didn't even realize I'd spoken aloud. "It was like this when we got here."

Flo and Otis had ascended to the flight deck through the hatch in the floor, which they'd accessed from the avionics section from beneath. The floor-hatch lock had long been broken, I know, because I was the one who broke it last year. Again, WorldAir did everything they were obligated to do in order to bring the interior of this plane to FAA safety standards for this trip to transition its sale to Peacock Airways—which is nearly nothing. A flight-deck floor hatch with a broken lock would literally never fly if this was a regular revenue route.

I was still confused over the disappearance of the cockpit crew, until Otis looked at me knowingly, then cocked his head toward the opening in the windshield. Suddenly it occurred to me. The two inertia reels—a system of cables and carabineers normally tucked inside the window frame—had been unwound and were streaming outside the aircraft. So the window had not been broken after all, it had been *deployed.* This was an emergency exit. The flight crew had bailed on the aircraft. This also explained the terrifying porpoising earlier, as a compromised aircraft would be expected to oscillate if the pilots did the unthinkable and just up and abandoned the wheel.

"But how . . ." I began. Otis shrugged his shoulders. Passenger airplane cockpits were normally not equipped with parachutes, but in this case, who knew. Though it would explain the curious descent I'd been noticing since soon after take off, before the gunshot caused the rapid decompression. That and the missing emergency raft from first class. If it was Ash's plan all along to parachute out of the airplane, he would have needed it to be at an altitude low enough for it to be safe to jump. I looked around the cockpit and, sure enough, the aircraft's positioning beacon was missing.

I donned the spare headphones and crouched behind Otis, as far from the open window as possible. "What's air traffic control telling us?" I tapped my headphones. All I heard was static.

"Nothing," Otis replied. "We lost contact with them awhile ago."

"What? How?"

Otis tossed me one of the counterfeit circuit breakers I'd handed him earlier. "It's a shortcut design, and faulty," he explained. "When the circuit pops it can't be reset, which not only blows out the communication system, but causes the cockpit to slowly depressurize."

My eyes widened with realization, and Otis nodded as if reading my mind. "What do we do?" I asked him.

"Not much we can do," he answered, and explained that debris from the aircraft cabin had been caught in two of the three engines, blowing them out, rendering them useless. The final engine was failing under the stress of the compromised aircraft, not to mention the porpoising we'd experienced earlier. As if on cue, another warning beep began blaring from the instrument panel, indicating we were about to lose the only engine we had left.

"Prepare the cabin," he directed me and Flo. Suddenly I cried out, remembering something.

"Wait! What about Grampa Roy?"

Otis shook his head. "I did what I could."

"What do you mean by that? How're they going to prove he's my grandfather?"

He nodded to Flo, who put her hand on my shoulder and said, "Kid, he's not your grandfather."

"What?" I screamed. But I'd heard her clearly, and there was no time for questions. Otis grabbed the microphone for the cabin PA system and spoke into it. "Ladies and gentlemen, please take your seats and secure your seatbelts," he intoned with the perfect public-announcement inflection of the seasoned pilot he never got to become. "We will be crashing shortly."

CHAPTER 22

Flo left the cockpit to brief the others, while I asked Otis how much time we had until impact. We were flying a few hundred feet above the ocean, which appeared calm, but from this distance a ten-foot wave would look like a ripple. Otis surmised we had six minutes until we ditched into the ocean. That might not sound like a lot of time, but it was enough time to categorize our situation as an "anticipated emergency"—which meant we could at least prepare ourselves somewhat for what was in store—as opposed to an "unanticipated emergency," which was a euphemistic-sounding category used for bombings and midair collisions and such. So, yeah, at least we had that going for us.

I returned to the cabin to tend to the others. Flo was briefing Malcolm and Anita, who had already donned their life vests, so I focused my attention on LaVonda and Officer

Ned. LaVonda had not only donned her life vest, but she had inflated it as well. I instructed her to take that one off and replace it with another.

"Why the hell I gotta take off a perfectly good life vest? At least I know this one here works fine. Look," she beat her fists against the vest, which bounced but stood up sturdily to the blows. I was hesitant to tell her why, but then figured this wasn't the time to coddle anyone.

"You can't inflate the vest until you're about to step out of the aircraft," I instructed her, "because otherwise, you know, if there's water inside the cabin, and your vest is inflated, you'll be floating up near the ceiling, making it harder to swim out."

Her eyes rounded with fear. I could see the seriousness of the situation sink into her. In my life, which admittedly was on the cusp of being a short one, I'd found that there are two levels of behavior in which people engage when it comes to panic. The first is that level you reach when you're afraid of heights or spiders or airplanes or whatever—sure, it's not illogical to be afraid of these things, but the odds are you're not gonna die by them. So my theory is that, at this level, people panic less out of real fear than they fear appearing like a fool for being afraid—the fear that, when all this is over, all that embarrassing loss of self-control was for nothing.

Then there's the next level, that level at which you finally understand, without a doubt, the direness of your situation. I assume, but I can't be certain, that soldiers experience this when they're about to charge into battle—the certainty that a percentage of them won't make it out the other side. At this level I think the panic is tamped down inside them, where it hardens like a fist, and instead of a loss of self-control there is the opposite—the resolute determination to focus forward, to make every move a concise one, to make it through.

I reached into the pouch under a nearby seat to grab a replacement vest for LaVonda, but to my surprise I felt something soft and furry instead. "Trixi!" I yelped, and pulled the shivering dog to my chest to give her a quick hug. LaVonda's face softened at the sight of the tiny pooch. I found another life vest and handed it to her. She put it on and left it uninflated.

Since Trixi was too small to actually wear the life vest, I inflated just one chamber of hers, placed a pillow in the center, and then put Trixi on top of that. I then wrapped the long straps of the vest around both the dog and the vest. The goal was to nestle her in the middle of a little flotation-device-like dog bed. I handed the whole lot to LaVonda, and I didn't know whether to be assured or worried in the knowledge that this woman would protect that sweet little creature with her life if she had to.

"Why not inflate it all the way?" LaVonda asked of Trixi's life vest.

I tried to smile reassuringly. "She weighs too little, you know, so if the ocean is rough, you don't want her too buoyant in the water." In other words, she could get tossed around and end up floating face-down otherwise. LaVonda's eyes widened, and the clarity of our situation set in again.

I saw that Flo was instructing Malcolm to likewise situate Captain Beefheart in his own life vest, so next I went to Officer Ned. He was breathing rapidly, and the new pillow had already soaked through with blood. I quickly replaced it with another one, draped a life vest over his head, then helped him secure the straps around his waist. I showed him the inflation tabs and told him to yank on them only as he exited the aircraft. Each vest contained small CO_2 canisters designed to immediately inflate the flotation chambers, exactly like the kind you find in automobile airbags.

I put my hand on his good shoulder and he put his hand over mine. Looking into my eyes, he smiled pallidly and said, "How many crashes does this make now, April? Five? You always make it through, April. Don't change now. Make sure you make it through."

I embraced him as best I could what with his shot-up arm and all, and assured him I'd make it through. I knew he was telling me to save myself, to not risk my safety for his sake. Despite my assurances to him, I could no easier leave him—or any of them—behind than I could perform eye surgery on myself. It wasn't in my nature. I'm sure it wasn't in theirs either.

Thus confident everyone was as best prepared for impact as one could hope, I kicked into gear. I had about four minutes to grab as many supplies as possible. I started by trying to gather more crew life vests, only to discover they were all gone from the front closet. I pulled what I could from under some seats and tossed them into the cockpit, along with the remnants of the emergency medical kit, the onboard defibrillators, and every flashlight from beneath every jumpseat on the aircraft. Next I grabbed Molly's large rucksack to gather more things. It was heavier than I remembered from back when I was trying to keep her from getting sucked out of the plane. But I was full of adrenaline then, as opposed to now, when the adrenaline had worked its way out the other side of me, leaving nothing but a simple resolution to complete each step as it came to me.

I stuffed a supply of Kotex from the lavatory into the bag (they make excellent bandages), then the soap dispenser, then the two rolls of toilet paper. I rifled through every galley cubby within reach of the cockpit, emptying them of anything that could remotely be of use: latex gloves, alcohol swabs, aspirin, Band-Aids, even an ancient jar of cocktail olives. I zipped the rucksack shut and clipped it to the D-ring protruding from the bustle at the right front door. This door would be our only option for an organized escape, as it still contained a slide raft engineered to deploy upon impact with the water.

Otis's voice suddenly blared over the PA system. "Thirty seconds to impact. Assume the brace position."

I stepped inside the cockpit, latched the door against the wall so it stayed open, then turned to look back at the cabin. It was this image, at this precise moment, that I swore I'd carry with me for the rest of my life, if there was even to be one. Each face before me—each dear face—ogled me with hope and fear. Anita held Malcolm's hand tightly against her chest, her cheeks stained with tears but her lips set in a firm line of determination. Between them lay Captain Beefheart, calmly wagging his tail under their protective hands. LaVonda gazed at me with heartbreakingly false confidence, as though attempting to comfort me—me, who got her into this and was keeping her from her home and loved ones right now. Tiny Trixibelle, attuned with canine intuition, shivered through her life vest in LaVonda's protective embrace. Officer Ned sat across the aisle from them, his head back, exhausted from loss of blood. He watched me through hooded eyes, his breath shallow. A smile softened his face. *What's that?* I wondered. Then it occurred to me. He was proud of me. This man, who could be in his executive office right now, polishing his prized motorcycle boots or joyously ordering people around, or with equal joy grumbling at LaVonda with false curmudgeonry, *was proud of me.* It was enough to make my heart break like a bone.

Then I looked at Malcolm. My best friend. He was such a good friend, in fact, that he reliably made me reconsider my lack of faith in humanity. If not for Malcolm I'd have probably been found face-down in a bathtub years ago. We were so different, the two of us—me the progeny of blue-collars, him of blue bloods—yet life without him would be inconceivable. He looked back at me with an expression weighted with guilt. Tears poured down his cheeks, and his shoulders shook. Anita patted his chest in an attempt to be comforting. Following her suit, I tried to smile at him upliftingly, but a sob caught in my throat instead.

Suddenly Flo appeared before me. "Kid," she said, embracing me briefly, "it's go time." She took her jumpseat, secured her safety straps, and began calling out her crash commands. *"Brace! Brace! Heads down! Stay low!"*

I hurriedly slipped into the captain's seat and strapped myself in. We were mere feet from the ocean. An odd thought entered my mind at that moment: *Wow, look how blue it is.* It was literally the color of my mother's eyes. Otis let out another hoot like this was fun for him, then turned to me and laughed, "You're my left eye, Crash!"

I felt the saltwater mist hit me through the opening in the cockpit window. Otis began the countdown. "Impact in minus five seconds . . . three . . . two . . . one . . ."

CHAPTER 23

The left wing was the first to break off. It hit a wave and took with it a large part of the starboard side of the aircraft. The sound was monstrous as the plane tore in half. Then the right wing sank into the sea like a keel at the bottom of a ship, briefly upending the remainder of the fuselage so that we hovered cruelly above the ocean before crashing back into it with the might of two planets colliding. I was alarmed by the sound of screaming until I realized it was my own.

"Brace! Brace! Heads down! Stay low!"

Then came the water. It gushed through the cockpit window with the force of a fire hose. I released my seatbelts and stood, only to have my feet slip out from beneath me as the flood of water carried me out of the cockpit and down the aisle.

"Release seatbelts! Get up! Get out!" I kept screaming. Flo was already out of her jumpseat opening the aircraft door. The slide raft should have been deployed as soon as the girt bar separated

from the door bustle. That was the point. It should have been automatic. But things rarely go as they should. Instead, water gushed through the opening, pushing the flaccid slide raft aside like it was a vertical window blind.

"Get up! Get out!" I couldn't even tell anymore if it was me or Flo screaming the commands, or perhaps it was the two of us now, one voice in unison. LaVonda sailed past me down the aisle, still clutching Trixibelle. I grabbed the collar of her life vest and held on. My foot gained purchase against a seat rail and I used my body to block the flow of any more people down the aisle. The point was to exit through the front forward door and into the raft, but I began to question this logic since the last I saw the raft didn't inflate.

An explosion deafened me even further. I realized it was the sound of the CO_2 canisters detonating the air into the raft. Flo must have found the manual inflation handle that is present on all slide rafts in the event they didn't deploy automatically. I felt a moment of relief only to be crushed again by the sound of LaVonda screaming.

"Trixi!" she wailed. The explosion had unnerved LaVonda and caused her grip to slip on the dog. Trixi yelped as she washed away from us and out the torn opening of the aircraft. "Trixi!" LaVonda cried again, reaching away from me toward the dog's direction.

"LaVonda, no!" I screamed. She was trying to extricate herself from my grip, trying to go after Trixi. "Please, don't." But it was no use. Within seconds she had writhed herself free and was washed out into the ocean after Trixi. I cried her name as I heard Anita and Malcolm cry mine. The force of the water was crushing. It pounded me like a ton of gravel as it washed through the fuselage. It was impossible to struggle against it to make my way toward the others, and just as impossible to keep my grip on the seat railing.

Suddenly I felt someone beside me. It was Officer Ned sliding past me down the aisle. He grabbed onto my waist with both arms. The weight of him forced loose my grip on the seat rail, and my fingers opened like reluctant flower petals. Soon we were both awash in the rushing water. It startled me that the cabin was completely submerged now, and here I'd forgotten to take a last gulp of air before going under. My lungs screamed in pain as we passed through the torn aircraft and into the open sea. When I looked above me I realized I didn't have near enough air in my lungs to last me to the surface. Even though Officer Ned gripped my vest with his injured arm and flailed toward the surface with the other, I knew I wouldn't make it. The last thing I remembered before feeling the water begin to fill my chest was the sight of the bottom of the raft as it floated what seemed like a mile above us.

Thank God somebody made it, I thought. Then the world went white.

CHAPTER 24

Southern Times

"Airline Heiress, Unofficial Mascot Among the Missing in Disappeared Jet"

April 4, 2014
by Clay Roundtree

It's either official or far from it. Whatever the case, the ongoing mystery surrounding WorldAir's disappearing airplanes took a new twist today when WorldAir spokesperson Rand Appleton confirmed reports that April Mae Manning, the temporarily deposed heiress to controlling stock in the company, along with the service dog Captain Beefheart, the airline's beloved unofficial mascot, is among those missing aboard WorldAir flight 9000 (also codeshared as Peacock Airways flight

0001), which disappeared over the Caribbean Sea two days ago after departing Atlanta Hartsfield International Airport for Grand Cayman. This brings the list of those passengers missing on WorldAir flights in the past year to a grand total of 272, a number that includes flight 0392, a 747 that vanished off the coast of Australia November 18.

This list remains frustratingly unofficial, though, due to the fact that one name on the passenger manifest—Morton Colgate—was discovered to belong to a body at the North Fulton County coroner's office that had been dead for days prior to the plane's disappearance. Another person on the departure report, crew member Teddy LaVista, was found to be alive and well and incarcerated at the Fulton County prison on drunk driving charges.

Appleton also confirmed that Ash Manning, April's adoptive father and the airplane's pilot, who had been in a raft off the coast of Cancún, claimed in his statement to the NTSB that he was the sole survivor of the L-1011 wreckage.

"His statement reads, 'Everyone else died on impact,'" Appleton said of Captain Manning's statement. "That is a verbatim quote."

Copilot John Dyer, a Grand Cayman national, was found floating in a life vest a half a mile away from the raft. He remains in a hospital in Cancún, Mexico, recovering from exposure and deep lacerations along his left thigh. Peacock Airways spokesperson Paul Packard reports that Dyer is unavailable to provide either a statement to the NTSB or a comment to the media at this time—other than what Dyer was recorded saying when the Mexican coast guard pulled him into the rescue vessel: "That prick Manning tried to feed me to the sharks!"

Dyer is not the only one skeptical of Mr. Manning's integrity, or his assertions regarding the survivors of the flight. The most vocal is Elizabeth Coleman, April's mother and Ash Manning's ex-wife. "Don't believe a word that bastard says," she insists of Mr. Manning. "Don't you dare stop searching the ocean for that plane! I know my daughter. I know she's alive."

The L-1011 aircraft, at the time of its disappearance, was being ferried to its new base in Grand Cayman after its sale by WorldAir to Peacock Airways. It vanished from the radar thirty-seven minutes after takeoff. At the same time all cockpit communication ceased. Search vessels from several countries were dispatched to an expanse of the Caribbean Sea between Cancún, Mexico, Nueva Gerona, Cuba and the Cayman Islands. The area was triangulated according to a radar blip believed to be the last captured from the injured aircraft.

Update: "Former WorldAir Pilot Ash Manning an FBI Informant"

5:16 P.M.

Ash Manning, the former WorldAir pilot pulled from the sea yesterday after losing control of the L-1011 passenger jet he was piloting, was revealed to be an FBI informant after documents and intercompany emails leaked to the media surfaced this afternoon. The emails detail Manning's FBI-sanctioned involvement with a suspected counterfeit airplane-parts smuggling operation headquartered in Atlanta in which a network of airline and airport employees were involved. The emails reference Manning's release from detainment after the crash of WorldAir's flight 1021 in Albuquerque last year, a condition of which was that he turn State's witness against those involved in the hijacking and further assist in the agency's investigation into the Atlanta-based smuggling ring.

In one email exchange between Manning and WorldAir CEO Vernon Wadley, Manning discloses that his ex-wife, mother of April Mae Manning, the teenager set to inherit controlling stock in the airline, had confided to him during their marriage that April was conceived via in vitro fertilization using donated sperm. This email is dated two days before April Manning was forcibly removed from the airline's executive offices pending confirmation of her lineage to late engineer/inventor Roy Coleman.

CHAPTER 25

The world was still white, and I still floated in it, but in a different way than when I was floating in the ocean. This world was warmer, for one, and so bright. I felt a familiar hand caress my face. I kept my eyes closed and smiled.

"Hi, Daddy."

"Hi, Goldie," he said. I felt him shake me gently. "Time to open your eyes."

I furrowed my brow. I didn't want to break this beautiful spell. It was bad enough I could already feel myself begin to sink back into the coldness that came before this moment. "No," I objected, "please let me stay."

He shook me a tad more firmly. His voice was sweet just like I remembered. "Time to wake up."

The shaking became frantic, the voice louder. "Wake up! *Wake up! April, please!* WAKE UP!"

I opened my eyes and the entire harsh, cold world seemed to empty back into me through my lungs. "Wake up," Malcolm sobbed as he performed chest compressions over me, "please, April!"

Flo stopped him—"She's back, Malcolm"—and turned me on my side. I coughed so violently it felt like I'd see my own socks fly out of my mouth any second. Once they were sure I'd expelled all the sea water out of my lungs, Flo and Malcolm helped me sit upright. I winced in pain. Malcolm probably cracked a rib or two. He was good at CPR; I knew because I taught him myself right out of the flight attendant handbook. Anita sat across from us in the raft, tending to Captain Beefheart, who was still strapped in his life vest contraption, and an exhausted Officer Ned. He caught sight of me, smiled, and in that second fell unconscious again. I felt bad he was always getting shot because of me.

"He'll be okay," Anita folded herself across his body to keep him warm and lessen his chances of going into shock. "He's breathing, he'll be fine. Yes," she continued, rubbing his forearms briskly, careful to avoid his bullet wound.

My throat felt like I'd swallowed a basket of sea urchins. "Where's LaVonda?" I craned my neck in a panic. Malcolm sat behind me, wrapped his arms around my waist, and pulled me to him. Flo sat in front of me and I wrapped my arms around her. There the three of us sat, front-to-back, like a shivering toboggan team. They still hadn't answered me.

"Where's LaVonda?" I repeated. "And where's Otis?"

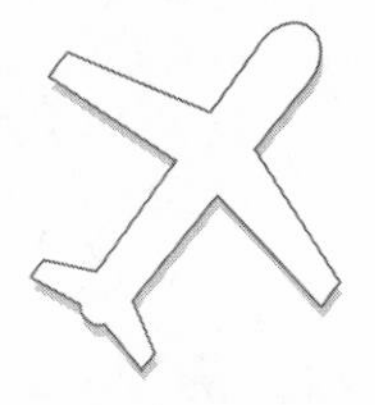

CHAPTER 26

Southern Times

"WorldAir Flight 9000, Bodies Identified"

April 4, 9:11 A.M.
by Clay Roundtree

Three bodies found floating in the Caribbean Sea were discovered by passengers on the Carnival cruise ship Exclamation! *earlier today. "I was showing my new bride how to flick bottle caps off the front of the ship and all of a sudden I says to myself, I says, 'What the hell is that out there floating in the ocean?'" passenger Mike Hammond recalls. "So I pointed it out to the cocktail waitress and she set out screaming for the captain."*

Floating in the ocean were three travel caskets containing human remains, each marked with stickers identifying them as cargo from WorldAir flight 9000, which crashed into the ocean two days ago. At a press conference held just minutes ago, search and rescue agency chief Fernando Montillo had this to say:

"The caskets contained the remains of three WorldAir employees, the identities of whom we were able to recover because of their work badges. Those identities are: Bus driver Whitney Smith, security officer John Parkerson and someone we believe to be a WorldAir mechanic. We actually found several different ID badges on that last one, so we picked the name with a picture to match his face: Otis Blodgett."

It was unclear if the victims perished as a result of the crash or had been in the cargo area being transported as human remains. "Well, since they were in caskets," Montillo said, "logic leads us to believe they'd been boarded that way, as human remains." Just then Montillo was taken aside by his assistant. When he returned to the microphone, Montillo said, "Ah, we have a survivor."

After the uproar quieted, questions arose as to where the search team found the survivor, to which Montillo answered, "I didn't say we found one. I said we have one."

Update EXCLUSIVE: "Body from WorldAir Flight 9000 Suddenly Springs Back to Life"

12:32 P.M.

Doctors, medical personnel and two passengers aboard the Carnival cruise ship Exclamation! *were startled speechless today when—after their ship was commandeered by an international search task force to temporarily store occupied caskets recovered from the wreckage of WorldAir flight 9000—a body inside one of the caskets suddenly sat upright and began howling like a wolf. Two nurses, an orderly and two passengers in the clinic waiting room immediately fainted, reportedly.*

"I could have sworn he was dead when he got here," says Dr. Veronica Li, communicating via her cellphone from the ship's hospital, where the formerly dead man had instructed her to call me. She reiterated, "That man looked pretty dead."

That man is Otis Blodgett, a WorldAir mechanic whose presence on board the doomed airplane was not documented on the passenger manifest and still needs to be explained. Blodgett tells this reporter, "Not dead, just rebooting."

Blodgett informs that he was in the cockpit at the time the plane crashed into the sea, at which point he got flushed through a break in the fuselage and out into the open water. "I just grabbed onto any flotation device I could find, and lo and behold"—his laughter does sound much like a wolf howling—"this casket knocks against me in the water. It's a perfectly sized little life boat, if you ask me."

Update: "WorldAir Flight 9000; Five Survivors, Plus One Dog, Found"

3:24 P.M.

Guided by airline mechanic Otis Blodgett, who earlier had been mistaken for a dead body rather than a survivor of the wreckage of WorldAir flight 9000, search and rescue task force members spotted a large yellow raft eight miles off the coast of Cuba just moments ago. Inside the raft were five more survivors of the crash: Malcolm Colgate, 15, Anita Washington, 42, WorldAir shareholder April Mae Manning, 16, WorldAir head of security Ned Rockwell, 41, and WorldAir flight attendant Flo Davenport, 67. All but Davenport's name were absent from the doomed plane's departure report. Their presence on the aircraft has yet to be explained and constitutes a major security breach in the company.

"How should I know?" an exasperated Vernon Wadley, the recently appointed CEO of WorldAir, says of the security breach. "My head of security is on a raft in the middle of the ocean right now."

Also on the raft was Captain Beefheart, the beloved mascot of WorldAir, shown here in a picture with rescue workers appearing on naval helicopter pilot Tyrone Bradley's Instagram account.

"Look who we found floating in the ocean! #CaptainBeefheart," the caption read. The update has received over 700,000 hits in the last half hour alone.

Southern Times

UPDATE: "WorldAir Mechanic's Head Found, America's Most Wanted Molly Marichino (aka Molly Hackman, aka Molly Martindale, aka Molly Taguchi) Among Perished in WorldAir Crash of Flight 9000"

April 6, 2014
by Clay Roundtree

Molly Marichino, or Molly Hackman as she's been called of late, was known to collect men. At the time of her death, which occurred horribly and accidentally by her own hand when she shot out the window of a WorldAir jet during flight and was sucked though the hole and into the airplane's engine, she had been married five times. Not five consecutive times, mind you, but five times concurrently.

"To pigeonhole her as just a bigamist would be like saying O.J. was just a football player," says Detective Jeffrey Wilson of the Beaumont Police Department. (For the purpose of combining all her aliases, she will be referred to as "Molly" from this point forward.) In 2000, Molly had escaped the Beaumont prison system by murdering and then impersonating the prison nurse, whom she'd befriended. She's been on the run ever since. "Whenever the police got close, she seemed to disappear again," Wilson observed. "It's like she was smoke."

Molly's fourth marriage was to Archibald Hackman, a mechanic for WorldAir whose severed head was among the items recovered from a rescue raft containing five survivors of the crash into the sea of WorldAir flight 9000. The head was discovered wrapped in plastic inside a rucksack said to have belonged to Molly. No one on board the raft is responding to requests for an interview.

"It was all part of one of her scams," Wilson explained. In this case the scam reportedly involved a half-million-dollar insurance policy that Hackman was due to collect. The policy centered on a woman clinging to life at the hospital, and if Hackman was discovered to have died before she did, the insurance company would not be obligated to pay out a settlement, leaving Molly unable to access the funds herself. "I knew she was evil, but to chop off someone's head? That's despicable."

The woman in the hospital died this morning. Hackman had identified her as his wife Molly upon admittance, but police discovered the woman's true identity to be Matilda Marie Remington Colgate, the former wife of Morton McGill Colgate, the beleaguered CEO of Colgate Enterprises.

Morton Colgate was Molly's fifth husband. According to Wilson, it was a move that led to the man's demise, as well as to the crash of WorldAir flight 9000. "She got greedy, that one," says Wilson. "Even for her, that was greedy."

Mr. Colgate's body was recently found partially incinerated in the downstairs bathroom of the house in Alpharetta that he bought for Molly. The death is still under investigation, but Wilson is certain Molly, along with Hackman, the husband who was also her partner in crime, had something to do with it. "No doubt in my mind," he says.

Southern Times

Update: "Search for Last WorldAir Flight 9000 Passenger Called Off"

April 6, 2014
by Clay Roundtree

Moments ago search and rescue agency chief Fernando Montillo delivered the grave news that today he planned to cancel search efforts for LaVonda Morgenstern, the WorldAir trauma liaison lost at sea in the crash of WorldAir flight 9000. Shown below is a picture of Morgenstern taken last year upon her training-day graduation at WorldAir.

"It is with much sadness and regret . . ." Montillo began, but then, as often happens during these press conferences, he was interrupted with a touch on his arm by an assistant. After a few cursory whispers, Montillo returned to the microphone and said, "We have a body."

Asked to clarify whether it was a body or a survivor, Montillo bent to confer with his assistant again, then readdressed the room. "Both," he said.

Update: "This Casket Washed Up on the Beach of Jamaica—What Partygoers Found Inside Will Surprise You"

3:08 P.M.

Spring breakers on the sands of Jamaica were in for a start when a weathered travel casket washed ashore this afternoon on the beach in front of a four-star resort. When the bravest of the beachgoers opened the casket to look inside, he was surprised when a small puff of white fur flew at his face.

"I didn't know what it was," says Trey Whitfield. "It had tiny teeth and tiny claws—it was like an albino bat or something. It really freaked me out."

Whitfield had no choice, he said, but to swat the creature to the ground. At that point a voice came booming from the casket.

"Oh no you did NOT just hit Trixi. You did NOT!"

Whitfield and his friends fled in terror. But others went toward the casket to find a corpse and a castaway, both wearing life vests.

"Where's Trixi?" the voice called. "There you are!" The dog jumped back into the casket. The voice belonged to none other than LaVonda Morgenstern, a WorldAir employee believed to have perished at sea after the crash of flight 9000, and the body was that of Roy Coleman, the late genius engineer whose legacy is presently in dispute until DNA results confirm

the paternity of his granddaughter, April Mae Manning. Manning was set to inherit his portfolio, which contained controlling stock of the WorldAir corporation, until the newly appointed CEO put a stop to it by demanding a DNA test to assure her lineage.

Most people would be traumatized after spending nearly two days in a floating travel coffin accompanied by a corpse, but Morgenstern seemed to take it in stride once she was assured her friends had survived the crash and her family members were on their way to join her in Jamaica. "I'm alive, I lost ten pounds and I'm sitting at a Tiki bar drinking a pina-damn-COLADA waiting for my boss to get out of the hospital and come pick me up!" she said, laughing.

A child selling turquoise jewelry sauntered by and Morgenstern called him over. "I'll take it all, your whole supply, tell the hotel to put it on WorldAir's bill—thank you, WorldAir!"

CHAPTER 27

Southern Times

EXCLUSIVE: "WorldAir Survivors Finally Talk about Their Ordeal"

April 29, 2014
by Clay Roundtree

So far it's been a harrowing month for the seven heroes of WorldAir flight 9000, scooped from the waters of the Caribbean after their plane crashed into the ocean on April 2. Today I meet with six of them, pictured below gathered around survivor Ned Rockwell's hospital bed, for an exclusive Q&A. The seventh, Malcolm Colgate, was unavailable for comment today, and the others agreed to this interview on the condition his privacy be respected.

Clay Roundtree: *First, congratulations on surviving your harrowing ordeal.*

Flo Davenport: *[Laughing] Congratulations on your book deal about our harrowing ordeal.*

CR: *Thank you! How is Malcolm doing?*

Flo Davenport: *Not bad for an instant orphan.*

CR: *I understand he's accessed his father's Grand Cayman accounts and is cooperating with federal investigators to return the money.*

Flo Davenport: *Good kid, that one.*

Anita Washington: *Flo, put that cigarette out. This is a hospital room!*

CR: *Anita, is it true that the person who leaked the FBI documents and emails between Ash Manning and the WorldAir CEO is your son, a sergeant in the Atlanta police department?*

Anita Washington: *No comment.*

CR: *Ms. Manning, may I call you April?*

April Mae Manning: *I prefer it over "Crash."*

CR: *Do you have any comment on the allegations that WorldAir CEO Vernon Wadley was behind the counterfeit airplane parts smuggling ring?*

April Mae Manning: *No.*

CR: *Or that he bribed the pilots to crash WorldAir flight 9000 into the ocean in order to collect the total insurance money for the L-1011 aircraft?*

April Mae Manning: *No.*

CR: *Or the allegations that your stepfather, Ash Manning, stole your grandfather's body in order to halt the collection of DNA evidence because he's still considered by the court to be your custodial parent and therefor still stood the possibility to be the executor of your inheritance?*

April Mae Manning: *He is not my custodial parent! That was just a filing mistake. My attorney is fixing it right now.*

CR: *I see that the status hearing is set for . . . next year?*

April Mae Manning: *Ugh! No comment!*

CR: *April, it must come as a relief to you to know that your inheritance was validated by the Supreme Court yesterday. The decision didn't come without its surprises, though. Your mother testified that your grandfather was the donor who provided the sample for in vitro fertilization, and her testimony was confirmed by DNA analysis. So your* *grandfather was really your father. What are your thoughts on that?*

April Mae Manning: *My grandfather was my* grandfather. *I had a father, his name was Robert Madison Coleman, and he was my father no matter what scientific tests you want to perform. And I loved them both—so much . . . I'd gladly sacrifice every cent of my inheritance to spend another minute with either of them.*

LaVonda Morgenstern: *Girl, you know it. I ain't even related to my babies by blood, but they's my babies. Ain't no test on earth to tell me otherwise. It ain't about tests. It's about* love. *Love is a bond you can't break. Your daddy loved you, your granddaddy, too.*

Flo Davenport: *They were both amazing men, Crash.*

Ned Rockwell: *Now we know where you get your brains.*

CR: *Mr. Rockwell, when are you expected to get out of the hospital?*

Ned Rockwell: *Who knows. I should just rent a room here. [They all laugh.]*

Otis Blodgett: *Ned, did you get the good painkillers? You need morphine and Percocet.* Combined. *I tell you, that's the stuff. Where's the pump? I told them to give you the pump.*

Ned Rockwell: *I don't need any more painkillers.*

Otis Blodgett: *I meant for me. Don't be selfish.*

CR: *Mr. Blodgett, why were you absent from the mayor's ceremony awarding you citizen of the year for your part in breaking up the smuggling ring and solving the mystery of the disappearance of WorldAir flight 0392? All the others were there, including Malcolm Colgate.*

Otis Blodgett: *I had to get the dent in my steel plate popped out. I kept shorting out and having to reboot. The other day I woke up in a pen at the zoo surrounded by pygmy goats.*

April Mae Manning: *How's that any different from a normal day?*

CR: *Seriously, Mr. Blodgett, you were the one who connected the counterfeit plane part as a faulty breaker that causes decompression and cockpit silence. Based on your calculations, the search and rescue task force has been redeployed. Yesterday they discovered a small piece of the wreckage off the coast of New Guinea. It's the first sign of the aircraft since last November 18, when it disappeared.*

LaVonda Morgenstern: *Ooh, you did NOT just say "aircraft" and "wreckage" in the same sentence. No you did NOT.*

April Mae Manning: *LaVonda, you* survived *a plane wreck! Nothing should scare you now.*

LaVonda Morgenstern: *I just don't like those words together in my head; they traumatize me. I wish sweet Mr. Beefcakes was here.*

CR: *Where is Captain Beefheart?*

April Mae Manning: *He's with Fifi Trixibelle at Malcolm's place. You can't separate those two.*

Flo Davenport: *[Laughing] That's not the only budding romance around here, is it, Thor?*

Ned Rockwell: *Stop it, guys.*

CR: *Right, Anita, from what I understand Ned has you to thank for keeping him from succumbing to shock while in the raft awaiting rescue.*

Anita Washington: *Yeah, well, I may be small, but I'm like a furnace when it comes to body heat.*

CR: *Flo, it was revealed last year that you are Ash Manning's biological mother . . .*

Flo Davenport: *I need a drink.*

CR: *. . . who put him up for adoption at birth . . .*

Flo Davenport: *Where's my flask?*

CR: *I was able to obtain Mr. Manning's actual birth certificate. Let me show it to you. It says here the father is . . .*

Flo Davenport: *Everybody cover your ears.*

CR: . . . *Otis Thelonius Blodgett*

LaVonda Morgenstern: *Uh oh, I think Otis died again. His good eye's gone all glassy.*

Anita Washington: *Get the defibrillators!*

Ned Rockwell: *Get the nurse!*

April Mae Manning: *I'll get the nurse.*

LaVonda Morgenstern: Otis! *You okay?* Otis! *Nurse! I'm sittin' here next to a dead man!*

Otis: *[Coughs] What dead man?*